The Playboy Pastor
Part 1: A Secret Romance

Written by: Andrea Furlow
Edited by: Opal Fox

Table of Contents

The Introduction

Life always came easy to James. His family was wealthy, he was tall, handsome, had a million dollar smile, and he's had the same smooth, Barry White voice since he was 14-years-old. And, oh how the ladies loved James. He never liked to keep too many women in his pocket. He was looking for his equal. He wanted someone who could stimulate his mind and electrify his body. That's what he found sexy. All through college, and even in his professional athletic career, James only dated a handful of women. Don't get it wrong, he had his share of one night stands, but he wasn't really seeking a wild sex life. He really only wanted one woman who could satisfy all his needs.

Thankfully dating wasn't a priority for James. Being an adored professional athlete was. He was addicted to the flashing lights and the fans screaming his name. He got high off the rush of adrenaline he felt while he played baseball. He loved the salty taste of sweat beading down all the canals of his body. He craved the feeling that his lungs could give out at any minute while he pushed his muscles to their ultimate limits. His life was one big battery that recharged every time he stepped onto the field. That's the way James liked it. That's the way James needed it.

But, like most professional athletes, retirement was inevitable. There was always some young punk who thought he was too cool for school, wagging his dick around in the locker room and making grandpa jokes. It was time for James to retire, but he didn't like the feeling of being forced out. Where would he get his adrenaline fix from? Who would be shouting his name and accosting him in the grocery store for an autograph? Sure, he'd still be famous, but not the level of fame he'd grown accustomed to.

The night before his retirement, James couldn't sleep. He lay in his bed and tossed around in the sheets. His body felt hot, then cold, then hot again. So many thoughts were whirling around in his head. Especially the thought of what's next. His mind hadn't settled on a new venture outside of sports. Plus, he was feeling the weight of being forgotten bearing down on his heart. It became very obvious that he wasn't going to get any sleep by the third time his body decided to turn into a sauna and burn him from the inside out. James decided to take a drive to wear down his mind and his body. His last game and retirement ceremony wasn't scheduled until 7:00 p.m., so he didn't need to sleep during the night. He could rest during the day and still kick ass on the field. He'd always been great like that.

James threw on a blue Nike sweatsuit, grabbed his car keys, and hopped into his gray Chevy Trailblazer. That's the car he liked to drive when he wanted to be incognito. No one ever wondered who he was when was in that car. It was a regular, non-flashy, mind-your-own-business type of car, and James needed that right now.

He drove around for what seemed like hours. He passed the baseball stadium with his picture and an advertisement of his retirement on the side. James just kept going. He drove far into the night. The lines of street lights seemed to pass him in a haze as he got swept into a trance. It was a freeing experience. James had nothing to do, no one to answer to. No one to entertain. It was just him and the road. It wasn't until the *ping* of the yellow gas light coming on in the car that James realized he wasn't paying attention to where or how far he'd gone. James looked round for a gas station and saw a 7-Eleven up ahead. He didn't really want to get out of his car, but the threat of not making it back home was enough motivation for him to stop. He pulled up to the pump and opened the door. The crisp taste of night air was sharp in his mouth as he yawned. He put one foot on the ground and realized he must have been driving for a while because his knee was stiff. He placed the other foot on the ground and stretched high in the air. His 6'2" frame, with arms stretched, towered over the car. He thought to himself, *James, let's get this gas and get out of here... And where is here?* James looked around for familiar surroundings but couldn't find any. He looked at the top of the building and saw the number 7704. He looked back at the street for a road sign. There was nothing. Confused, and starting to get a little sleepy, James walked around the car. As he walked, he patted his pockets. After the fourth or fifth pat, James realized he'd forgotten his wallet at home. He left the house without even considering if he had his driver's license or credit cards.

James walked back around to the driver's side door and opened it quickly. The second realization dawned on him that he'd left his cell phone at home too. James said to himself, *Damn man, you're 0 for 2 right now.* James climbed back into the driver's seat and closed the door. He gripped the steering wheel with both hands and rested his head on his hands in anguish. He had no gas, no money, no phone, and no idea where he was. He couldn't get help even if he wanted to. Just then, James heard *clink clink clink* on his window. It sounded like keys tapping. James lifted his head from the wheel and looked to his left. There he saw the most beautiful, tall figure standing at his window wearing a killer little black dress and a trancing smile. James couldn't hide his shock. His mouth dropped and his body didn't move. It was obvious he liked what he saw, which made the woman blush. She motioned for him to roll down the window. James complied.

"Hey. James, right?" James looked at her for a second, but he couldn't seem to get any words to come out of his mouth. She continued, "It looks like you need some help. Is everything ok?" James snapped himself out of the trance and finally closed his mouth. He felt his face flush. His mouth was open for so long it had actually become dry. He finally responded.

"Yes. I'm James. And you are?"

"Alice."

"Alice. Alice. That's a beautiful name." James extended his hand for Alice to shake. Just then they heard a scream. Alice and James both jump with fright. It was the middle of the night and someone was screaming. On the other side of the parking lot, two young women in their late teens or early twenties were looking at James' car, pointing, and screaming with excitement. They began to run over towards the car. James looked at Alice with a devilish grin and said, "This happens all the time. Excuse me." He motioned for Alice to move back so he could open the door. James pulled on the handle, but the girls got to the car a lot faster than he expected. He didn't want to open the door and hit them, so he let the handle go and sat back in his seat smiling. The girls were screaming inaudibly and jumping with excitement. James studied Alice's face to see if she was impressed by the fanfare happening before her, but she was actually blushing again. It wasn't until he looked at the girls' faces that he realized that they were there for Alice and not him. James was puzzled. What was happening? Is it possible that this impressive woman is more famous than him? Finally, James asked, "Who are you?"

She smiled at him and said, "I'm Alice." James returned her smile and examined her face. She enjoyed the attention she was getting. Although she didn't anticipate anyone recognizing her at a 7-Eleven in the middle of the night, it was a welcomed surprise. The ladies finished taking their pictures and hugging Alice and ran back to their car across the lot.

James opened his door and got out of his car. He had to see Alice up close to know if the perfection he saw through the window was real or a facade. As he stepped closer, he noticed Alice was just an inch or two shorter than him with her heels on, which meant she really was much taller than the average woman. He looked at her delicately manicured toes that introduced her long, tan legs. She had clearly been exposed to the sun and it had kissed her skin to the point where the color now had a permanent glow. And, she was wearing that dress like it was painted on to cover just the legally required parts. Her makeup was light, and natural. She didn't need to be caked up because she was naturally beautiful. Lastly, James loved how many teeth she used when she smiled. He thought about how easy it would be to know what she liked and what amused her by her smile. If he had to pick out a flaw, her hair was too short for his liking. He loved women with long hair. Not that her chin-length bob was unattractive, it was lovely, but just not his preference.

"Well, Ms. Alice. What is a beauty like yourself doing out this late?" He stepped closer to Alice but not too close as to alarm her. He wanted to get to a distance where she knew he was interested but far enough away to feel safe.

"I was just named to the USA Women's Olympic Volleyball team. I was celebrating with my new teammates." James nodded his head in approval.

"Wow, and a world famous athlete? What else can you do?" Alice chuckled.

"Fly a plane." James' jaw dropped in shock.

"No way!" James exclaimed. "Really?"

"No, not really. I'm just messin' with you." Alice stepped up to James and lightly pushed him in the breast plate. James stumbled backwards dramatically and clutched his chest.

"I'm suing you for assault before my last game. You must have a boyfriend on the opposite team." Alice smirked at James knowing he was fishing for information.

"Nope, no man on my arm. I haven't found a guy who can deal with my busy schedule or lack of privacy. Unless. . ." Alice cut off her words abruptly and pointed her finger at her chin in a thinking motion. "Well how does your girlfriend deal with all your fame?" James doubled over laughing. He found himself loving every minute of their interaction. Alice had a sense of humor which was sexier than her slim figure and collected persona.

"I see what you did there. I'm definitely single. But, maybe not for long." James flashed Alice a sexy smile with a raised, inquisitive eyebrow.

"Slow down there, sir." Alice put up hand to gesture a stop sign. "How about we start with dinner and see where it goes from there." James nodded in agreement.

"Sure. How about this? My game should be over tomorrow at like 9:30 p.m. Maybe earlier with some good pitching. I can take a shower, do a little press, and be ready for a late dinner around 10. Would you like to come to the game and leave with me right after?" Alice thought for a moment and smiled with all her teeth. James knew a yes was about to follow that smile. He was learning her mannerisms already.

"That would be nice. But listen, dinner is on you. Looks like I'm about to pay a grip for your gas tonight." Alice laughed. James had gotten so wrapped up in the conversation with Alice that he forgot he was stranded at a gas station far from home. He looked at his watch and realized it was truly time to get home and rest. The hard part was over. James had piqued Alice's interest and she agreed to go out with him the next night. That was his accomplishment for the evening, so there was no need to draw out the night any further.

"You're right." James responded. "I'll have to find a place worthy of my hero. Medieval Times?" Alice pushed passed James, hit him with a hard shoulder to shoulder, and walked over to the pump. She tapped her card on the reader, pushed a few buttons and returned her credit card to her clutch bag. She opened the gas cap of James' car, inserted the gas nozzle, and set the hands-free latch. James thought she was going to come back to conclude the conversation, but she turned the opposite way.

"I'm positive you'll think of something better." Alice called to James over her shoulder as she walked to her car. He was impressed by her brand new black Audi. She got in the car and drove off. She disappeared just as quickly as she had appeared. James couldn't believe he had met one of the most incredible women he'd ever seen. He knew she was going to be truly someone special to him. Just then, the gas pump clicked to signal it was full. James returned the pump and collected the receipt. He was starting to feel sleepy, which was a great sign, and so he climbed into his car and drove in what he believed to be the direction of home.

"Alice." James whispered with a smile. "I could get used to that."

****

The next afternoon, James woke up feeling refreshed. He had slept through the team's morning workout after being out so late the past night. All he could think about was getting through the game to start his new civilian life, and that began with a late night dinner with Alice. He put his phone on the charger when he got home, but he forgot to turn it on. James powered up the phone and walked into the restroom to relieve himself. He could hear the phone dinging with messages as he washed his hands and returned to it. Most of the messages were from coaches and teammates, so he ignored them. The last message was from his public relations agent. It read *Who is Alice?* James opened the message with the cheesiest grin, but he couldn't begin to reply to such a loaded question. *Who is Alice?* James thought for a second before his fingers subconsciously took over the

10

conversation. *Alice is the perfect stranger my soul didn't know it needed to meet last night. I didn't even catch her last name, but I know she's going to be my wife.* James waited for a second for a reply. Then, his phone dinged. *Wow! I guess that's a yes for putting her on your guest list for the game. I can't wait to meet the future Mrs.*

James dropped the phone on his bed and half skipped back into the bathroom to get dressed. He needed to hightail it to the stadium if he was going to warm up properly. One of the reasons he was retiring was his body's fair warning that it was time. He'd come out lucky to never have more than an ankle sprain in his career, but his body was beginning to feel the strain from the stop and start motions of the game. James washed his face, brushed his teeth, and threw on a sweat suit. He grabbed a protein shake from the fridge and headed towards the garage. All his keys were by the garage door. He had a decision to make. If he wanted to impress any other woman, then he would take the Porsche. But this was Alice. She wouldn't be impressed by a car, but rather she'd be impressed by his class. So, James grabbed the Range Rover keys and hit the button to open the garage. His phone notification went off one more time. *Looking forward to tonight* came from an unknown number. *Alice.* James thought as he pulled out and onto the main road.

James beamed all the way to the stadium. Not even realizing he didn't respond to Alice's text, he couldn't stop thinking about how a chance encounter could change his whole perspective on his retirement day. The day became hazy. Sure, James changed into his uniform. Sure, James warmed up. Sure, James had the retirement game every baseball player dreamed of with a grand slam to win the closely scored game at the bottom of the ninth. Maybe it was a softball pitch to set him up for a successful sendoff, but nothing could shake the floating feeling under James' feet. To date, it was the best 24 hours of his life.

Once the game was over, James rushed into the locker room to shower and change for the press conference. He was looking forward to one last post-game press frenzy. He put on his finest suit and styled his hair in a way he knew the cameras and Alice would love. It was going to be his last post-game in this locker room, so James took a moment to look around. All of the memories and friendships he had made in that room were coming to an end. Of course, he would come back the next day to collect his belongings and say goodbye to the team and staff, but this was going to be the last time he would be a part of the jubilation of a win with his team. It was a moment James savored as he inhaled deeply and physically felt the energy in the room.

James sat in his locker stall and checked his phone to see if he had gotten any messages from Alice during the game. He knew she was in the stands, and that was his subconscious motivation to play harder. He never spotted her during the game, but from the four messages from her, he knew she was cheering him on. The first message read *I'm here. Good luck tonight.* The second read *Wow! That was amazing.* The third read *Ok, that was a turn on,* adorned with a splash emoji. The last read *Congratulations! What a spectacular win. I'm going to head down to the press room to wait for you. See you soon.* That last message was just what he needed to cement that moment for the night. James was floating on a cloud. He could feel the butterflies floating in his stomach, and he knew it was time to receive his final hurrah. He had the heck of a game, so James walked into the press room with confidence knowing all eyes and cheers would be for him. To his surprise, he got nothing. The press was in fact in a frenzy, but it was all for Alice.

"Alice, Alice, they say this is Team USA's best chance for a gold medal in women's volleyball. Is this our Olympic year?"

"Alice, Alice, Alice. Over here."

"Alice, what brings you here tonight? Who are you here to see?"

Alice finally realized James walked into the press room. She smiled at him apologetically and walked towards the back of the room. "The man of the hour is here." As Alice motioned towards the tabletop podium, the reporters turned around to see that James had entered. They immediately turned their attention to him. James didn't know how to feel. He wasn't used to coming second to anyone. Alice was just as beautiful as she was the evening before. He loved that she showed up for his big day but felt conflicted about how she garnered just as much, if not more, attention than him on a day that was supposed to be all about him. James shook out the negative thoughts trying to intrude into his mind. It was his moment again, and that was all that mattered. Maybe there was a little fragility to his ego, but that wasn't going to stop him from savoring this moment. It was his time, and

Alice was there to witness him in his last moment of baseball glory. James felt invincible.

Andrea Furlow

The Decision

It was an easy decision to marry Alice. James had finally met his equal. She matched him in every way. They had the same business mind, the same financial status, their conversations stimulated every part of him, she was smoking hot, and her sex drive rivaled a twenty-year-old frat boy. James couldn't get enough of Alice. So, when it came time to lock her down, James knew what he had to do.

James was originally from Milwaukee, Wisconsin. He was born and raised in the Fox Point neighborhood, and his parents still maintained his childhood home there. Alice didn't really have a home. She was an Army brat who moved around a lot growing up, so when James suggested they move to Milwaukee after retirement, Alice had no disagreements. She loved James and James adored her. She knew James wouldn't do anything to hurt her, so she trusted this decision completely. They were happy to share their lives together in a place they could call home.

Two years after getting married, James and Alice welcomed twin sons. James affectionately, and ironically, called them Teeny and Tiny. For twins, they were big at birth, and since they were breast-fed babies, they plumped up even larger after a few months. Fatherhood had its challenges, but James was able to find his rhythm quickly. So quickly that two years later, James and Alice welcomed another set of twin sons. James affectionately called them Eyes and Ears. They were quiet children, but they watched and mimicked everything their older brothers were doing. Although Alice's athletic body was able to bounce back quickly after having children, she didn't want to have any more. She officially closed the baby factory and asked

James to get a vasectomy. With their family complete, James and Alice enjoyed a quiet life in Fox Point for the next 10 years.

James and Alice were happily married, they'd managed to raise four polite, respectful, and strappingly handsome young sons. Alice loved being a boy mom. She enjoyed the constant adoration from her sons. Being the only woman in the house, she constantly had "fans" to rave over her. Any boy mom could tell you, that after the formative years are complete, a mother's role turns into the best time of her life because she gets to truly enjoy her sons while dad's role becomes to launch the boys into men. Alice's role as a mother would never be over, but her time and hard work on the frontline had ceased and she could take a backseat in raising her boys while James took the wheel. She was exactly where she wanted to be.

On the other hand, it took James a while to figure out what he wanted to do with his life after playing baseball. He and Alice made excellent investments with their retirement monies, so there was no rush into an actual career. They were enjoying the retirement life, but James was starting to feel like something was missing. He couldn't quite put his finger on the ever-growing void. Some days he'd sit back and watch as Alice rolled around on the floor with the boys. He'd watch her make funny faces at them and laugh so hard that the veins in her forehead would begin to protrude. Everyone seemed so happy. James was happy too, but he wasn't the kind of happy that they all were. Something wasn't quite right in his life. There were months that would go by that James couldn't remember what he did or where he went on a given day. James felt like he was sinking into more than a rut, so he decided to see a therapist.

He didn't want to alarm Alice, so James didn't say where he was going on the day of his appointment. He just said he was heading out and he'd be back in time for dinner. Alice loved and trusted her husband, so she kindly kissed him goodbye as he walked out of the door. James slid into his sleek new, blue BMW and slowly pulled out of the driveway. As he was driving, James contemplated what he was going to say to this perfect stranger. He didn't feel depressed. There was a lot of joy in his life. He didn't feel anxious. He just felt like something was devoid from his perfect life. He wanted the therapist to confirm he was ok. Maybe even come up with a solution to what didn't really need to be labeled as a problem.

The drive was only about 15 minutes to Dr. Michaels' downtown Milwaukee office. James valeted his car out front and handed the girl a $50 tip. "Keep it close." He said as he winked and grabbed the valet ticket out of her hand and continued to walk past her. He could tell the girl was looking at him with attraction and was impressed by the tip. James loved those looks. He was confident that he could still pull any lady he wanted to, but he didn't want to. Alice was his perfect match. He just liked to know that he still had *it*. James walked into the glass building and headed straight to the elevator. The building's lobby was bright, lustrous, and airy. It reminded James of the stadium lobby where he used to play. Suddenly and profoundly, it hit James. He missed the roaring fans and the gleaming, bright lights of the stadium. That's what was causing such a lack in his life. James pushed the elevator button, but he wasn't sure if he still wanted to go see Dr. Michaels. He'd figured out what was missing in his life, so did he really need to go see a therapist? What was this guy going to tell him now that he'd figured out what the so-called "problem" was? James turned to walk back towards the exit when the elevator door dinged. The doors began to open and he heard his name.

"James?" James turned around to see a tall and handsome man standing in the elevator. It was Dr. Michaels. He was an older man, seemingly in his late 50's or early 60's, but you could tell he was in great physical shape by the way his tailored gray suit fit him to a tee. His hair was perfectly cut and sculpted, and James was impressed by the way he pieced himself together. He spoke again, "James, I thought that was you. Where are you going?"

James thought for a second of something to say that would make the embarrassment less awkward, but he figured the truth would be the best in this situation. "I was having second thoughts about seeing a therapist. To be honest, I had an epiphany as I walked into the building, so I really don't think I need to go up to your office." Dr. Michaels raised his eyebrow.

"Oh really? An epiphany? Listen, why don't you tell me about your epiphany in the elevator on the way upstairs. If you're sure you don't want to talk by the time we get to my office, then there's no charge and you can just ride the elevator back down. No harm, no foul, and you'll make it back before the free 30 minutes expires on your valet. Sound like a deal?" James nodded in agreement and both men got on the elevator.

"How did you know I was here?" James asked.

"I give the lobby receptionist a picture of all my clients. When he sees them arrive, he buzzes my personal receptionist. This way I can greet all my clients in the lobby. It's a personal touch I like to provide. Plus, I work with many former athletes like yourself. It gives me a chance to run them down when they look like they're about to change their minds about coming to see me." James laughed.

"Do you get a lot of runners?"

Dr. Michaels chuckled to himself. "More than you know." He then pressed the 30th floor button and the elevator doors closed. "So, tell me about this epiphany." James took in a deep breath as he began.

"I have the perfect life. I have a beautiful wife, I have great kids, my home is one of the best in the neighborhood, my parents and siblings are very close, so we have a great village to support my family. I've just been feeling like something is missing. It wasn't until I walked into your lobby, which reminded me of my old stadium, that I realized I missed playing ball. Now that I know what's wrong, I can fix it. I really don't need to talk it out. I'm sorry to have wasted your time." Dr. Michaels listened intently as James told him about his so-called epiphany. He then responded.

"I think it's great that you realize what was causing you to have an empty feeling. But, I'd still like for you to come to my office. You've recognized the what, but now you need to figure out the how. I'd like to work with you to figure that out. You see, I'm a former athlete myself." James cut him off.

"I knew you looked familiar. You were one of my favorite football players growing up. Aw man! What an honor to meet you." James reached out and shook the doctor's hand vigorously. Dr. Michaels continued.

"Nice to meet you, too. To be honest, you were one of my favorite players as well. But I think I know what you're going through. We have to figure out what happens after they turn off the stadium lights on our careers. The 'what's next?' question becomes too much for some people to handle."

"That's true"

"I'm glad you agree. But it's not just enough to agree. Not many people know what it's like to be in our shoes. You'll bounce an idea off of them and they'll look at you like you have two heads. I believe my office can be a safe space for you. A place where you can tell me your ideas without judgment. What do you think?" James leaned back on the elevator rail while he thought. Just then the doors to the elevator opened on the 30th floor. Dr. Michaels got out of the elevator and turned around. He placed his hand on the elevator opening so it wouldn't close. James rubbed his chin in submission and got off the elevator too.

The 30th floor was surprisingly bright. The hallway was lined with green tinted windows. Although you couldn't see through them, you could hear people talking within them. There was the smell of fresh coffee in the air. It felt as if there was business being conducted, but they were only in the hallway. Dr. Michaels' office was at the very end of the corridor. James could see the brown door with *The Office of Dr. Michaels* written on a gold placard towards the top and centered. Dr. Michaels let James lead the way. It felt like Dr. Michaels was subconsciously letting James choose to walk through the doors of his office. Like it was an actual choice. Although there wasn't a blue pill or a red pill to swallow, James did feel like he wanted to get to the truth of his existence after his professional sports career. James grabbed the gold, moon-shaped door handle and pulled it. He held the door open for Dr. Michaels to enter after he walked in.

Inside the door was the reception area. To the right, there was a long, black sofa. It looked uncomfortable. As if to say, you won't be in this area for too long, so don't get cozy. To the left, there was a glass receptionist desk. A slender young man with chestnut brown hair and blond highlights sat behind the desk wearing a headset. He had a donut in his right hand and a pencil in his left. He was talking into the headset. When he looked up and saw James and Dr. Michaels coming through the door, he quickly told whoever was on the phone he'd call them back, dropped the pencil and the donut, and clumsily stood to his feet. He nodded at Dr. Michaels and addressed James. "Good afternoon Mr.-" James held up his hand to say *pause* and interrupt.

"Just James is fine." The receptionist nodded in response.

18

"Right. James. Would you like some coffee or a water?" James shook his head, mouthed the word no, and flashed a smile with gratitude. The receptionist continued, "Please let me know if you change your mind. Dr. Michaels, your usual is on your desk." The receptionist sat back down. Dr. Michaels hurried past James to another large door. It wasn't marked, but it was presumably Dr. Michaels' actual office. This door had the same gold, moon-shaped handle. Dr. Michaels pulled the handle and opened the door for James. James was immediately impressed with the panoramic, round office. It was truly on the 30th floor with views of the entire downtown area on one side and the most pristine view of Lake Michigan on the other side. James mouthed the word *wow*.

"Doc, I've got to say. You must be doing some great work up here. This view says it all." Dr. Michaels responded.

"We do ok." He walked towards the windows and around his executive desk. He grabbed the coffee mug on the edge of the desk and sipped the contents. He half choked on the beverage before he took a hard swallow. "Jesus! How can this kid be so terrible?" James looked at the doctor with a puzzled face. "I'm sorry. That kid, the receptionist, he's my daughter's boyfriend. He's the worst employee you could ever ask for, but I can't fire him. It would break my daughter's heart." James laughed. Dr. Michaels continued. "I asked for black coffee with two sugars and a sprinkle of cinnamon. There's more creamer in this coffee than coffee." James laughed again.

"I'm glad I'm not there yet. My oldest twins are 12 and the youngest are 10. All my guys will be in middle school in the fall. I'm not ready for real life favors and consequences just yet." Dr. Michaels laughed and responded.

"You'll be here before you know it. Why don't you have a seat?" Dr. Michaels' open hand and extended arm guided a path towards two armchairs in the corner of the office by the window. The oversized and very comfortable chairs face each other with a small, round coffee table in between. With James' large frame, he doesn't always get to sit this comfortably, so he felt at ease in the chair. It felt like the chair was saying, *kick back old friend,* and James obliged. Dr. Michaels led the charge. "So tell me, James, what could you imagine yourself doing for the next 50 years? I know you don't *have* to work, but you do want to do something. What could that 'something' be?"

James pondered the question for a moment. No one had ever asked him what he wanted to be in life. The assumption was always that he was going to be a professional athlete. He was destined for and achieved athletic excellence, but that all ended years ago. With his retirement money and the investment money constantly flowing in, he never had to worry about being financially stable after ball. It was that nagging feeling of not having a purpose, that was driving the decision to find a life outside of sports. His family was great, that wasn't ever in question, but there was an element of joy missing from James' life. Alice found joy and purpose in being a mother. And she was damn good at it. James knew he was a good father, but that didn't bring him joy or excitement. The question was eating away at James. Which must have shown through the expression on his face because Dr. Michaels began to wave his hand back and forth in front of James' face to get his attention. "Where did you go?" he asked. James replied.

"That's such a tough question, doc. Most people get asked that question at 5, and they answer, 'a policeman' or 'a doctor.' My answer was always a pro ball player. I didn't know which ball it would be. I was naturally gifted in all sports, but I knew I'd make it. I maintained the same answer year after year, decade after decade. The crazy part is, no one ever told me I couldn't. Everyone supported me 100%, without question, I was gonna make it. No one ever told me to make a plan B. And here I am now in my mid 40's and I'm being asked what I want to be when I grow up, and I have no clue." Dr. Michaels nodded with understanding as James talked. James liked the feeling of being heard and that someone wasn't judging him for not having all the answers. Dr. Michaels responded.

"James, I apologize if I made you feel like you had to give me an answer in the moment. I wasn't looking for a concrete response. Let me rephrase the question. What is it that you're missing from your game playing days that you want to recreate in your post-game days?" James knew that answer right away.

"It's the spotlight. The thousands of eyes eagerly waiting to see what I'm gonna do next. I would be ok with a few people chanting my name." James chuckled to himself. Dr. Michaels chuckled a little too. He motioned for James to continue. "Yeah,

I'd love that element of live entertainment." Dr. Michaels interjected.

"Ok, so something in the entertainment industry. Maybe like a sports analyst or a commentator?" James rebutted immediately.

"No, definitely not an on-camera personality. Those guys have to watch what they say. It's easy to get canceled in this day and age."

"So then do you have any talents? Can you sing or dance? Are you the next Mick Jagger?" James open-mouth laughed at that thought. "Ok, I see I'm way off base here." Retorted Dr. Michaels, as he reached for the notepad sitting on a nearby table. "Let's try an exercise. Let's make a list of all of the professions that meet your qualifications. You make a list, I'll make a list, and we'll put them in an envelope. Take the weekend to enjoy your family and friends, but don't think about your future at all. This'll give you time to clear your mind. Then on Monday, open the envelope and see if anything jumps out at you. By then you should be open to whatever grabs your heart. And if nothing does, then we'll meet again next week to dive deeper into other possible solutions or professions. Can we do that? Does that sound like a plan?" James nodded in agreement.

"I can do that."

Dr. Michaels handed James a sheet of paper from the notepad. He looked around for a pen, but he only found the one he kept in his jacket pocket. He pulled the pen out for himself, but then he realized James would need one too. Dr. Michaels stood up and walked to his desk. There was a round, tall container with several pens, all in black ink. He grabbed one, along with an envelope that was loose on his desk and sat back down. Then he reached across the coffee table to hand both to James. James had already begun to think of the professions he could stand doing. Just to be clear, James asked, "So just write down anything." Dr. Michaels responded immediately.

"Anything you could see yourself actually doing. Don't write *"Cirque Du Soleil Acrobat"* if you don't want to wear tights and you're afraid of heights." Both men laughed.

"I got ya, doc." James looked at his blank note paper. For some reason, he felt excited. It was a blank slate. He could become whoever he wanted to be. He could reinvent himself a few times over, but what he was really excited about was the possibilities that come with a fresh start. To him, it was like going on a first date. You could be dining with the woman of your dreams, or the devil incarnate. Either way, you'd have to actually be brave enough to go on the date to find out. The corners of James' mouth rose and fell several times. He was going to have to write something down. He stared at this blank paper for another second and then he looked up to see what Dr. Michaels was writing. Dr. Michaels shifted in his seat when he saw James try to peek at his paper. "Come on doc, you not gonna let me even peek?" Dr. Michaels didn't respond. He just smirked a little and kept writing. James looked back down at his paper, tapped the pen in his right hand with his index finger, and finally put the pen to paper. "And so the journey begins," he said as he began to write.

****

James loved Sunday nights. It was the only night of the week that he was guaranteed to have some alone time with Alice. The boys all went to their rooms early to get ready for school the next day and to finish any homework or projects they'd put off until the last minute. Alice looked forward to it too. Sure, they'd sneak into the laundry room or duck into the shower for some intimate time during the week, but it was known throughout the household not to disturb mom and dad on Sunday nights unless the house was on fire. And even then, let the smoke detectors alert them. James called it the *don't knock* rule. It was just about 9:00 p.m. when James heard the last bedroom door close. He knew no one would be coming out of their rooms for the remainder of the night, so he hurried throughout the house to look for Alice. He wanted to take full advantage of the hours of uninterrupted privacy they'd now been afforded by the Sunday night ritual. He checked her second floor office. No Alice. He peeked around the corner into the loft. Still, no Alice. James was a little confused, so he walked back into their bedroom. Maybe she'd started without him, he thought. Nope, no Alice. Finally, James walked downstairs. He heard some movement coming from the kitchen, so he headed that way. As he made his way down the corridor, he saw there were still lights on in the house. As James began turning off the lights he said, "These damn kids keep leaving all these lights on. No money for the bill, but no time to turn the lights off." As he fussed and walked, he had to snap himself back into his mission. He wanted to find his wife and get their night started.

"James, baby?" James knew that *baby* from anywhere. He knew that was the sexy beckoning of a woman who wanted him. He could hear the lust in her voice, and he knew there was some kind of surprise waiting for him when he found her. James walked through the kitchen threshold, but Alice wasn't there. He could have sworn he heard her call from the kitchen, but she wasn't in his line of sight. "Babe?" There she goes again. James turned towards the sound of her voice and this time it was coming from the living room. James tiptoed towards the living room thinking he could surprise his wife and literally sweep her off her feet. But when he got to the living room, Alice wasn't there. By now James is a little confused. His wife is definitely playing a seductive game, but he wasn't catching on to what the game was. He'd happily chase her around the house, but he couldn't find her to chase her. Just then he heard the *sexiest* sound in his world. The sound of high heels going up the hardwood staircase. James loved a woman in high heels, especially his wife. He loved that the heels made her 6-foot frame tower over him. They made her legs look like they alone were 6-feet long. James could feel his body start to get warm. Each step made him feel an extra twinge of desire for his wife. He didn't want her to reach the top of the stairs. He wanted that sound to last, but inevitably it didn't. He could hear the heels going down the hallway and then he heard the door to his bedroom close. That was James' cue to make his way upstairs.

There was a flickering glow coming from underneath his bedroom door. James knew this was from the candles Alice liked to keep around the room. Alice had a sex *tell*. Whenever she wanted to make love, she'd light a candle. It could be upstairs, downstairs, in their bedroom or in any random room. When Alice lit a candle, that was her clue to James that she was in the mood for his lovin'. To see the flickering light got James even more aroused. Even after all the years of being married, Alice was still the only woman that James ever really desired. It was more than desire. He craved to be close to Alice. She always smelled like she'd just gotten out of the shower and her skin always tasted like raw honey. Alice was the only woman that could satisfy James' desires all in one place. Every part of being with her was exhilarating. Then tack on the fact that he got to make love to her, and James was right at home.

James opened their bedroom door to find his naked wife wearing his favorite blue tie and a matching pair of stiletto heels. She was standing next to the tall dresser across the room with her legs crossed at the ankles. One arm was bent at the elbow and resting on top of the dresser. She uncrossed her legs and stood up straight. She stroked James' tie with both hands as she walked across the room towards him. The candle flames danced across her body as if they were just as pleased as James was at this moment. James opened his arms to draw his wife near, but she walked around his hands and to his back. Alice walked behind James and put her bare breasts on his back. She reached around him and hugged his chest. James put his hands over hers, but Alice pushed them off. James loved when Alice was forceful with him. He was always in control around the house, but the one place he liked to be completely submissive was in the bedroom. And Alice had a way of knowing the right balance of taking charge while also letting James control his climax. This made James want to please her even more.

Alice kissed the back of James' neck, which sent chills down his spine. James turned around and faced his wife. He kissed her lips gently, but Alice backed away immediately. "Excuse me sir, you're not paying me to kiss." she whispered. James was completely erected by her words. Alice reached down and unbuckled his belt. James was eager to help his wife take his pants down, but she slapped his hands away. "Slow down baby," she whispered sweetly, "Candy is here to take care of all your needs."

"Candy is it?" James inquires. "I'm a happily married man. I don't usually take home strange women. I'm not sure if I want to do this." Alice pulled down James' pants and underwear in one full motion. She then got down on her knees in front of James.

"I won't be long, baby." Alice said as she took James' fully engorged member into her mouth. James moaned with pleasure as his wife studied every part of his flesh. He didn't know where

24

she had gotten her skills and he didn't care. He was in total ecstasy as she licked, flicked, and stroked him into submission. Alice could sense that James had gotten too far into the oral love by his sputtered breathing, so she stopped. She stood to her feet and helped him pull off his t-shirt; James then stepped out of his pants and underwear, leaving on his socks. James reached out and grabbed his wife by her waist, drawing her near. He pressed her body up against his and kissed her lips passionately. As much as Alice wanted to stay in the role, her husband's strong hands made her give way to his will. Alice made one final attempt to push James back, but it was too late, James had assumed control of her playful act. He swiftly raised her off her feet, so Alice wrapped her legs around his waist. James turned towards the bed, but he changed his mind. He placed his wife on the chase at the foot of the bed and let her go. He got onto his knee. He wanted to return the mouth favor, but Alice stopped him. She grabbed him by the hand and pulled it down to her triangle. She let him feel just how excited she was. It was then that James felt a rush of adrenaline to his heart. There was no containing his excitement. He climbed on top of his wife's frame and entered her with the ferocity of a man who was in love and lust at the same time. Alice pushed her face into James' chest to contain her moan. They both knew their children were aware of the activity going on in the bedroom, but they knew they shouldn't confirm the common knowledge. They quietly gave into each other completely and became one flesh. It was their happy place, their happy moment, and it was perfect.

James enjoyed waking up to his beautiful wife. He loved how she smelled of honey the morning after sex. He couldn't explain it, but she smelled and tasted so sweet. As if her sweat was made by the gods. He would bottle it up and sell it if he could. This was a special morning. Waking up next to his love and opening the envelope from his Dr. Michaels visit was all that was on his mind. James slid his arm from underneath Alice's naked body. He tried not to disturb her as he went to the bathroom. He thought, looking at his erect penis, how nice it would be for a quick round two this morning, but the hustle and bustle of the household would pick up any minute now. Even though the boys were old enough to get themselves ready for school, Alice insisted on being a part of their morning routine. She made breakfast they'd barely eat, packed them lunches and snacks that they'd give to the kids who forgot their lunch money or liked what Alice packed better than what their mothers packed, and kissed them all goodbye. That part they loved. All Alice's sons were mama's boys. They couldn't get enough hugs and kisses from their mother. She didn't baby them, Alice knew they were young men, but she had never and would never stop showing them love and affection.

Once the boys were out the door, James went to get the envelope from his coat pocket. He successfully retrieved the envelope and went to Alice's office where he knew she would be. Alice didn't need an office, but it was her safe space in the house. There, she could check the family finances and investments, watch the trashy reality TV shows the boys never wanted to watch with her, and journal her thoughts away. It wasn't often she'd *need* to go into her office, but she would go there after the boys went to school as a part of her daily routine.

"Knock knock." James said as he peeked his head into the doorway. Alice looked up from the computer. She was sitting behind the desk with a plain white v-neck t-shirt and some purple plaid pajama shorts. She didn't need reading glasses, but Alice always wore screen protector glasses when she worked on the computer. She said the screen light hurt her eyes. "Can you help me with something?" James asked.

"Of course, my love. What's up?" Alice replied. She smiled warmly at James as she motioned for him to come over. James entered the room with hesitation. He knew this would be the first day of a new beginning. He'd anticipated opening the envelope for days, but he was more afraid that Alice would reject the idea of him starting a new venture and shaking up their perfect lives. James approached her desk and handed Alice the envelope. "What's this?" Alice asked. James rubbed his chin in hesitation. He didn't want to answer, but he knew he had to.

"I went to see Dr. Michaels. You know, the therapist the league recommended for after I retired?" Alice had a surprised look come upon her face, but she nodded as if she was following the conversation. "So, he suggested that we both write down a list of potential professions for me to try out now that I'm retired." Alice shook her head in confusion.

"Honey, I don't think I'm following you. You're looking for a job? And why do you need a therapist to help you find a job?" James smiled and held his hands up in submission.

"Ok, let me start from the beginning. I went to see Dr. Michaels last week. I was having an empty feeling that I couldn't put my finger on. When I walked into the lobby of his office building, I realized that it looked like the lobby of my old stadium. I figured out in the lobby that I missed the feeling of being important." Alice interrupted.

"You don't feel important?" James could tell that he wasn't explaining himself very well, so he sat down and leaned across the table to get closer to Alice.

"Of course, I feel important to this family. But I'm missing the sense of being important in other people's lives. I was in their living rooms every week. Sometimes, multiple times a week. I was on their lips almost every day during the season. They heard my name on the sports shows. I miss feeling the spotlight. That's what I mean by not being important. I want to feel like I'm making the world smile again." Alice smiled with sympathy for James. She knew how he felt. She was, in fact, a former professional athlete too. Actually, she was a more famous professional athlete. She enjoyed the feeling of entertaining the world too. But she loved being a mom even more.

"I get it babe, if anyone could understand, it'd be me. I wish you would have come to me first. Why did you feel the need to go to a therapist? You didn't think you could trust me with this?" James felt embarrassed. He didn't even consider talking to Alice.

"I'm sorry babe, I wasn't really thinking about it like that. It's not that I didn't trust you. It's just that I didn't think about you." Alice threw her hands up as if to say, "that's fucked up." James realized then he, in fact, had fucked up. "Wait, that's not what I meant. I just meant that I was in my feelings. I wasn't thinking about anyone else because I was only thinking about what I was feeling." Alice put her hands down and leaned forward to listen more intently. "I realized in that lobby that I wanted to do something that I felt would bring me that attention again. I love our quiet life here, but I know I'll never truly feel fulfilled until I fill that empty place in my heart. I love you more than Pull-n-Peel Twizzlers at the movie theater, but I know that I can't be the husband and father you need me to be if I don't become a whole person again." Alice nodded with understanding.

"I get it. You know I do. So then what's in the envelope?" Alice holds up the envelope.

"It's a list of the things I could do in my retirement." Alice looked puzzled again.

"Why do I need to open it?" She asked

"Because I haven't seen the second half of the list."

"Babe, you're going to have to make a little more sense. I'm trying to be supportive and understanding, but I feel like I'm missing the whole story here." James took a deep breath before he answered.

"Dr. Michaels wrote a list of potential professions, and I wrote a list of them too. He said we should put them in an envelope and not look at them until Monday. That way I could look at the list with clear eyes and possibly pick a profession off the list." Alice nodded as if she understood.

"Ahhh, I get it now. Ok, so you're nervous about what's on his list. Ok. This is starting to make sense now. So, you want me to open the envelope and do your dirty work for you. No sir! You got yourself into this mess. You'll have to get yourself out of it." James looked at Alice in shock.

"You not gonna help out your husband?" James quipped. Alice outstretched the envelope in James' direction for him to take.

"Nope!"

James reached out and snatched the envelope from Alice's hand. Alice took a playful swing at James, but she missed as James recoiled quickly.

"Fine! But I'm going to remember that the next time you want some of this sweet lovin'. I won't be so willing to put out." Alice smiled.

"Stop stalin' fat boy!" James laughed and nodded as if Alice said something that was true. James looked at the envelope for a second. Alice could tell he was still hesitant to open it, so she handed James a letter opener. James took the letter opener out of Alice's hand. He flipped the envelope over and opened the back with the letter opener.

"Here goes nothin'." James pulled out both sheets of paper. He handed one to Alice. "You take this one, and I'll take this one." Alice took the paper and nodded in agreement. He then stated,

"You go first." Alice gave James a sly smile.

"Fine! I'll go first." The tan paper was folded in thirds. Alice unfolded the paper, looked at it, and looked up at James inquisitively. "There're just squiggly lines on this one. What am I missing?" She held the paper up so James could see it. He laughed.

"That was mine. I didn't know what to write." Alice and James both laugh as he continued. "I went there for someone to help me solve a problem. Not to solve it myself. I'm the customer." Alice then leaned forward and looked down at James's folded paper in his hands still resting in his lap. James saw where her eyes went and realized it was his turn. "I guess it's my turn, huh?" James lifted the paper and unfolded it. His heart started to beat faster. His palms felt a little shaky. How could he be so nervous about something he didn't know he cared about so much? James looked down at the paper.

"What does it say?" Alice asked. James sat in silence for another long pause. "Babe?" James looked up at Alice and held up the paper for her to see. Alice read the words on the paper in her head. She couldn't wrap her head around the words. Alice opened her mouth to speak, but her mouth seemed to go dry. "A…a" Alice rewetted her mouth and cleared her throat. "A Pastor?" She asked. "Is this a serious suggestion?" Dr. Michaels had written only one profession on the paper. Underneath, he explained why he chose the profession. He wrote:

> I want you to be open to this suggestion. It may not have been something you've considered before, but here's why I think it'll fit you well.
> 1. People adore pastors.
> 2. You get to "perform" weekly.
> 3. If you pick the right denomination, then they can cheer you on.
> 4. You'll have an instant following because of your fame.
> 5. Pastors, especially megachurch pastors, make a lot of money.

James sat back in his chair. He let the letter fall into his lap and he put his hands over his face. He wiped his face from his forehead to his chin and then stood up. The letter fell to the floor as James turned and walked out of the room. Alice was left in her office chair in shock. She didn't want to follow her husband. She knew he needed space to process what he'd just read, but she needed time to process what she'd just read too. Was she going to be a first lady? Did she really want James to put her family under such scrutiny? She would have to put on the heir of being the perfect wife and mother. It wouldn't just be James under the microscope, but it would be her and her sons too. Alice turned and looked out of her office window. How could she focus on what she was doing after this kind of news?

Alice curled herself into a ball in her chair and continued to stare out of the window. Her thoughts then drifted to her childhood. As a girl, Alice remembered going to church every Sunday. It all seemed so fake to her. She recognized how hypocritical people were from a young age. She hated how her mother put on a fake smile and fawned over the first lady. Her mother hated the first lady because she'd stolen her boyfriend in high school. Yet, her mother sang this woman's praises every Sunday. In her religious traditions, and growing up in her household, the men made the decisions while the women supported their husbands. She knew what she had to do, which was to support her husband, but she had to reconcile in her mind *how* she wanted to support her husband. As she peered out the window, she fell into a trance. It was the same place she went in the last hours of natural childbirth when she saw, heard, and felt nothing.

As James left Alice's office, he knew he had to get a drink. He walked into the kitchen and opened the refrigerator. He studied the drink options in the refrigerator and then closed the door. There was nothing there to quench his thirst or his questions. So then James went two cabinets to the right of the fridge, the liquor cabinet. He pulled out the bottle of Crown Royal Peach and a squat glass. He set the bottle on the countertop and then returned to the refrigerator door with the glass to get ice out of the dispenser. He then went into the refrigerator again and poured sweet tea from a gallon jug to fill up the ice glass halfway. Finally, James returned to the Crown Royal bottle, opened it, and filled the glass the rest of the way. He shook it around a little to mix the drink. The sound of the ice clanking against the glass was soothing for James. It sounded like liquid relief was coming. He took the glass into the living room and sat on the couch. Normally, James would turn on the TV and sip his drink slowly as he watched a sporting event or some mindless TV, but James wasn't in the mood to do anything but think. He took a long swig of his drink and set the glass on the end table. James could hear his mother's voice yelling, *Get a coaster!* So, he reached to the back of the end table, retrieved a coaster from the stack, and placed it under his drink.

It wasn't that Dr. Michaels had given him a profession that he hadn't thought of that bothered James. It was the fact that it was a good suggestion that bothered him. Being a former athlete himself, Dr. Michaels knew all of the emotions that former athletes go through after retirement. James couldn't imagine a former athlete steering him wrong. Plus, he loved the idea of being in bright lights and getting weekly adoration again. He also loved God. That was an important part of the job. His hesitation was that he didn't experience the same "calling" that people talked about when they decided to go into ministry. He knew he had a knack for entertaining people. He also knew his former fame would bring in the men and his beautiful features and sexy baritone voice would bring in the women. Dr. Michaels was right, he would have an instant following. It was, in fact, a great idea. James sat on the couch in silence. He had to think this through. Was he going to make this decision to turn his and his family's lives upside down to pursue his fulfillment? Or was he going to keep looking for something else? James decided he couldn't make this decision alone. He wanted to talk to Alice, but he was afraid she would try to talk him into or out of the decision.

He knew he needed to talk to Dr. Michaels again. James could never find his cell phone when he needed it. James patted his pockets. No phone. He looked around the room. No phone. James then saw the cordless phone across the room. Alice insisted they'd gotten an alarm system when they moved into the house. She was afraid that their high profiles would invite thieves to invade their home. He was grateful at that moment that his wife insisted on the alarm system that required a landline. He was also annoyed with his wife that she wouldn't let them upgrade to the system that only required the internet. James grabbed the drink and took another long sip as he lifted himself off of the couch and walked towards the phone. James lifted the phone off of its base with one hand and continued to hold his drink in the other. He pressed the on button and began to dial Dr. Michaels' phone number. The phone began to ring. It rang once and James took a sip of his drink. It rang twice and James took another sip. It rang a third time, and as James went to take a sip, Dr. Michaels answered.

"Good morning. This is Dr. Michaels." James' heart stopped. He had expected the receptionist to answer the phone so he could make an appointment. He wasn't anticipating Dr. Michaels himself.

"Good morning sir. This is James um… James." Why was James so nervous? He knew Dr. Michaels was anticipating his call, but he just wasn't expecting to be talking to him so soon after he saw the doctor's suggestion. "I wasn't expecting you to answer the phone." Dr. Michaels giggled before he responded.

"Yes. Well, that's what happens when you employ your unemployable, future son-in-law. Sometimes you have to answer the phones when he takes a bagel break that lasts an hour. I'm happy to hear from you, though. I'm assuming you read my list." James suddenly remembered why he'd called.

"Yes sir. I read it. That's why I'm calling. I wanted to schedule a follow up appointment." James could hear the hesitation in Dr. Michaels' voice.

"No you didn't." James was confused. He thought that was the plan. He thought he was supposed to read both lists and then schedule a follow up appointment with the doctor to discuss the professions and to decide if they'd be a good fit. What was happening? Why would the doctor not remember the plan? James replied.

"Excuse me? I thought we said I would…" Dr. Michaels cut him off.

"What I mean is, you're not coming in for a follow up appointment to talk through my suggestion. You're coming in for me to explain, and possibly convince you to take, my suggestion. What I wrote down is for you to contemplate with yourself, your wife, and your kids. Once you've talked to them, then we can schedule an appointment. But something tells me you won't need to schedule that appointment. Something tells me you've already decided what you want to do and you're just looking for validation. I can give you that over the phone right now. You don't need to drive all the way down here for me to tell you the same thing I'm going to say right now. James, it's the right move for you. Let go and let God. Isn't that how the saying goes?" That wasn't the reaction, or the conversation James expected to have with Dr. Michaels. But the doctor was right. He knew when he unfolded the tan paper, heck, he knew when he met him in the lobby, that Dr. Michaels was going to have the right answers. James was looking for his purpose, and Dr. Michaels found his personal calling through therapy. It was an easy choice to take the advice of a man who was walking in the shoes that James wanted to walk in.

"You're right. Thanks for your time, doc. I'll talk to my family." James hung up the phone without saying goodbye. He knew instantly that it was time to go talk to Alice. James finished his drink in one, large gulp. He deposited the glass in the kitchen sink on his way to Alice's office. He dreaded the idea that Alice would disagree with his decision, and it would tear their family apart. It could have been how quickly he'd ingested his Crown Peach Tea or the idea of him possibly imploding 14 years of marriage that made James sick to his stomach as he walked down the hallway. Either way, James didn't feel well. As he reached the door to Alice's office, he could see her sitting in the same spot where she was when he left. Alice was still curled up in her office chair, looking out of the window. James knocked softly on the door. Alice looked up at James and smiled. She had a huge tear in her eye. It didn't look like she'd been crying, but Alice's watery eye instantly broke James' heart. "My love?" James said, as more of a question than a statement. Alice's tear fell as she answered.

"We'll need to move to the Bible Belt if we're going to make this work. Choose a city with a lot of attractions, a sports team or teams, and an A-rated school system, and I'll explain it to the kids." James' jaw dropped. Alice continued as another tear fell from her eye. Her voice was unwavering as she said "And James, this better not change you. It better not change us." Alice turned back to the window as more tears fell from her eyes. James turned and walked away. There was nothing left to say. Alice had already solidified the decision. They were moving to the Bible Belt.

The Move to Charlotte

James couldn't believe the response he'd gotten from just one month of marketing. The sanctuary was packed to the brim with fans and churchgoers alike. There had to have been at least a thousand people in the church on the first Sunday of Mount Ebenezer Bread of Life. James felt a lump in his throat as he sat behind his desk in his office in the back of the church. He could hear the music of the praise and worship team playing at a distance. Public speaking was never his forte, but James knew he had to make this work. Alice was gracious and never complained about the move to Charlotte, North Carolina. Even the boys were excited about a new adventure. But, the pressure to make sure he succeeded was weighing heavily on James' thoughts. His first sermon was masterfully crafted, so it wasn't the pressure of performing well. He knew the sermon would be well received. It was the thought of being able to sustain this lifestyle and to keep the people happy for a lifetime. Suddenly, there was a knock at the door. James didn't realize he was in a haze until the sound broke him out of it. He looked up to see Alice's smiling face. She could tell he felt the pressure. Alice knew her husband very well. Somehow, she always knew exactly what to say, when to say it, and how to put James' mind at ease. Alice walked over to her husband and kissed him on the forehead. James wrapped his arms around Alice's waist and pulled her closer to his body. He kissed her lips softly. At that moment, another knock came to the open door. "Pastor, we have about 10 minutes before you and First Lady need to be seated." Saul was the deliverer of the timing news. Saul had become a good friend to James. He was the first person James hired as a pastor's adjutant when they first purchased the church building.

Saul was an Air Force veteran. He took pride in his work, he guarded James' time and privacy, and made sure to be a loyal friend and assistant. That's why Saul was invaluable to the transition to Charlotte. Without him, James would be lost. So, when he appeared in the doorway with the 10-minute warning, James adhered to his word.

"We'll be there in a minute." Alice answered Saul. She gave him a nod, and Saul closed the office door as he backed out in a bowing and humbled posture. "Husband, I know today is a big day for you."

"For us." James interjected.

"Yes, for us. But, I want you to be at ease. Those people showed up for you. I know you have a word for them but let me encourage you first. You're a great man, a powerful speaker, and everyone will love you. You just need to show them your heart, and they'll follow your lead." James smiled at his doting wife. He loved how Alice always made him feel better. "And if that doesn't clear your mind, then maybe this will." Alice put both of her hands on James' chest and pushed him back into his chair until his back was resting on the seat. James was pleasantly surprised at this unexpected, yet intimate moment. He could feel his heart rate quicken and his blood rush downward. She lowered herself onto the floor between his legs and rested on her knees. She then reached down to unbuckle his pants. James grabbed her hands with delight, but with hesitation.

"We only have about 10 minutes. What you doin'?" James looked at the sinister look on his wife's face. Again, typical Alice. She knew exactly what James needed, even if he didn't ask for it. Alice pushed James' hands out of the way.

"Then I guess I better work fast." She took out his rising gourd through the slit in his underwear. James was already turned on by the surprise of his wife's gesture. Alice lowered her puckered mouth towards his manhood. She took him into her mouth in a long, swallowing stroke. James could only show his excitement on his face. He knew he couldn't let the sound of his pleasure escape because of the abundance of people in the church. He was positive Saul was standing guard outside the door, but who wants to see the first lady on her knees on the first day of service. Alice was swift and intent on pleasuring her husband. She pulled out all the stops, knowing all of James' pleasure points, it didn't take long for her to look up and see her husband's signature eyebrow raise as he ascended into Heaven. Saul lightly tapped on the door. A quick swallow, and Alice was on her feet and adjusting her nylon stockings back under her knee-length skirt. James tucked himself away and stood up next to his wife.

"Showtime, pastor." Saul whispered through the door. James kissed his wife on the cheek. Checked himself out in the mirror on the office wall and walked towards the door. He grabbed Alice's hand on the way to the door. They exchanged loving glances as James opened the door by the silver knob, and walked into what was sure to be his destiny.

As the door opened, Saul, who was wearing a security earpiece, tapped the button to speak. "All call and respond. Pastor and First Lady are on the move."

"10-4." Replied four male voices on the other end. Saul led the way down the corridor that led to the sanctuary. The entrance from the back of the church led directly into the side entrance of the pulpit. The area was clear. James took one last breath as Saul opened the curtain to the pulpit. He and Alice walked through the curtain, hand in hand, as they both put on their million dollar smiles. To James, it was just like the introductions on gameday. Like walking out of the dugout and onto the field. As soon as he came out of the shadows, the spotlights from the roof shined bright. The entire sanctuary went stark raving mad. The people cheered loudly as if they were at the stadium. This was how he used to feel every week, so to relive the feeling again was exactly what James was looking for. He craved the attention, starved for it in fact, and the satisfaction of feeling adored again made James feel the dopamine rush again. He and Alice waved as they walked across the pulpit stage to where their sons were sitting. James ensured Alice was seated. He kissed her on the hand and let it go. James then fist bumped each of his sons, and then turned towards the podium. He put his arms out as if to present his family to the church, and the crowd cheered louder. James had a strut to him that day. He knew his Word was going to send shockwaves through the church, so he was almost cocky as he walked to the podium.

"Welcome!" James shouted into the microphone attached to the podium. Again, the crowd went bananas for their pastor. He then pulled the microphone from the stand and adjusted the cord.

"Praise the Lord, saints." He said as he continued to adjust the cord so as to not trip on it. The crowd responded with the same statement. "I said, praise the Lord, saints." Hallelujahs rang out across the sanctuary. "Welcome to our first Sunday service at Mount Ebenezer Bread of Life. On behalf of my family and myself, I'd like to personally welcome you to our service. I have a Word for you today, and what a Word it's going to be. Amen?" Amens rang out across the sanctuary. James looked out at all the faces of the people in the crowd. They seemed totally engaged in his every word. James could have told them to get naked, and they would have joyfully complied. This was it. James took a deep breath. He felt his mouth get dry. Just as he was turning to look for Saul to bring him some water, Saul was already there standing beside him with a glass with a napkin covering the top. It wasn't that he was psychic, but Saul, like Alice, had a way of anticipating James' needs. This wasn't his first time being a pastor's aid, so the experience of anticipating the pastor's needs came with the territory. James took a sip of water. "Saints, before we begin, let's go to our Father in prayer. Bow your heads, and let's go humbly before the Lord." James bowed his head and so did the rest of the church. "Lord, we welcome you into this place today. May Your words flow through me and may they be received by Your people. For it is in Your name that we gather here today. We thank you in advance for the life-changing, earth-moving, and powerful Word You're going to deliver through me today. It's in the name of Jesus we pray, and let all the saints of God say…"

"Amen."

Just as he thought, James was a natural. The sermon went over well, and the people were fully invested in his words. It was just how James had imagined it would be. Alice and the boys were impressed at how James talked *to* the people rather than *at* them. He made the language plain and spoke about wealth and prosperity. That's something that the fire and brimstone pastors in the area lacked. He knew this sermon would lure away other parishioners. A message of hope always resonated with the people of the area, so he catered to his niche market.

James stood in the doorway of the church and greeted the attendees as they exited. He was determined to stay as long as it took to make sure he said a heartfelt *thank you* to all who were in service. He wanted to appear close and available, even though he knew in the back of his mind he had hired an amazing staff to handle the daily operations of the church.

A younger man, about the age of 30 approached James. "Pastor James, you made my heart smile today. I'm just so happy you moved to our town. All these preachers around here just want to collect money and make you feel bad, but you made me feel good today. I'll be back next week." James smiled and responded.

"Hey brother, that's what I'm here for. You don't have to wait until Sunday. We have Bible study on Wednesday nights."

"I can't promise you that." The man responded. Just then a beautiful woman walked by and smiled as she lowered her head with a humble blush on her face. The man followed her with his eyes.

James laughed audibly. "Alright, I'll see you on Wednesday."

"Sure, sure, pastor. I'll see you on Wednesday." The man replied as he pursued his target down the corridor with his eyes. It was apparent James had lost this new patron's attention, so he continued back towards his office to retrieve his things and head home for the day.

James was tired. He'd given his sermon his all. As the people kept calling back in encouragement, James got deeper and deeper into the emotional impact. It took a lot out of him. He wanted to take his family out to celebrate, but he was too tired. Also, Sundays used to be the day that he and Alice were intimate, but between the oral gift she'd given him before church and the sermon, James just wanted to go home and rest. James waited until the last person was out the door. He looked back and located Saul. He gave him a wave as he gathered his brood and walked out the door. James could count on Saul to make sure the church was locked up properly, so he didn't worry as he pulled the keys from his pocket and walked towards one of the last cars in the parking lot.

At home, James sat in his recliner with his feet up. He had a notepad on his chest, a pen in his hand, and his signature Crown Peach Tea on a coaster, sitting on the end table next to the chair. The television was tuned into a football game. Although James loved football, he didn't have a favorite team. He just enjoyed watching whatever game was on. Now that his first Sunday had gone off without a hitch, James wanted to gameplan what he wanted the church to mean to the community. He knew that it wasn't enough to just open the church doors on Sundays and Wednesday. He had to get people to invest into his plan and his vision, but what was that vision going to be? How could he set himself apart from the other pastors in the area? Sure, there were enough people so each pastor could have their share of members, but if James was going to live a millionaire's lifestyle in Charlotte, then he would need a megachurch. Not just any megachurch, but one with at least 10,000 members. The piddly 1,000 was ok for the first Sunday, but James needed a plan to get to 10,000. That was his magic number. With that many members, he could buy a stadium-style church.

James reached for his drink and took a sip. He put it back down and lifted the notepad off of his chest. It was time for James to make a list of all of the things he wanted to do in the community to attract attention. What could he do? James thought about all the things his professional team did in the community. They had food drives. James wrote "food drive" on his notepad. They had toy drives. James wrote "toy drive" on his notepad, but James wasn't satisfied with these thoughts. Everyone did food drives. Everyone did toy drives. James didn't want to be like everyone else. He wanted to stand out. James knew he couldn't go at this alone, so he enlisted the help of Alice. "Babe!" James called into the other room. "Babe! Come here a sec." James yelled. Alice came walking around the corner with a towel in her hands. It looked like she was drying dishes, but James couldn't tell what she was doing. "You busy?" James asked.

"No. I was just finishing up the dishes. The boys are doing homework. What's up?" James held up his notepad.

"I'm trying to come up with some unique, signature initiatives for the church. I want our causes to stand out. You know, bring in members who want to support us and our causes." Alice looked up in the air as she thought of some ideas.

"Oh, you remember those pampering sessions for single moms we did with my team. We would get them massages, mani/pedis, hair treatments, and watch their kids while they got pampered? Then at the end of the year, we'd raffle off a car to one of them. That's unheard of around these parts. What do you think?" Alice could see the excitement and the wheels turning in James' head. "I'm guessing you like that idea?" James smiled.

"That's a great idea. We would bring in a lot of single moms. That would also attract a lot of men looking to 'date' those single women." James held up air quotes as he said the word date. He knew Alice knew what he meant. Alice walked over and slapped him across the legs with the towel in her hand.

"You're not here to pimp out the single women in the community." Alice commanded. James recoiled.

"I'm not trying to 'pimp out' these women." James held up the air quotes again. "I think the church is a great place to meet your mate. Wouldn't you rather people meet in the church than in the club?" Alice thought for a moment.

"Yeah, I guess."

"What else you got?" James asked

"You got the usual suspects: toy drives, backpacks at school time."

"Oooooo, backpacks." James commented as he wrote it down on his list.

"You've got family and friends days and festivals. Let's see. You've also got to think of putting people to work. There's an entire vacant shopping center next to the church building. Well, mostly vacant. The coin laundry seems to have survived up until now. There's no reason why the church doesn't buy or rent that space for businesses. We could have a barbershop slash beauty salon, a thrift store, a restaurant, and a counseling office." James held his hand up as if to say that's too much. Alice could tell she was losing her husband, so she continued through his objection. "Wait, hear me out. The church is supposed to be a beacon of hope for the community. Let's say a family's house burns down. They could come and get clothes from the thrift store, food to eat from the restaurant, and Christian counseling from the professionals to deal with the trauma of it all. Let the Red Cross or United Way help them rebuild their house, but we could be there for them in a small way. Or let's say they need help paying a bill. The church will pay the bill, but they have to volunteer at one of the church's businesses. We get free labor, and they get the help they need. Remember back in the day when the pastor lived next door to the church? If the people needed a place to stay, they'd stay with the pastor. If they were hungry, they could get a meal. If they needed counseling, then they'd seek out wise counsel. Why couldn't we be that for the 21st century? But, instead of them coming here, they'd go to the church office, and they'd hook them up with whatever they need. This would set us apart from these other churches. We'd be a community church. The more money we make, the more we could do to impact the community."

James sat up in his chair. "Woman, you are brilliant!" James exclaimed. "I knew you were beautiful, I knew you had brains, but you're truly the ultimate idea spot. That's exactly what this community needs. And that's what'll get us to 10,000 real fast." Alice looked at James puzzled.

"What's 10,000? Dollars?" Alice asked.

"No. Members. 10,000 members." James said as a smile came over his face. Alice was even more puzzled.

"Where did you come up with that number?" She asked.

"I'm just trying to turn dollars into cents. If we had 10,000 members, and everyone gave $10, then we'd make $100,000 per week, conservatively. That's $5.2 million dollars a year, tax-free." Alice's confusion was starting to turn into anger.

"Are you looking for the money or the impact? I thought you wanted ideas for community impact. Not for the money." James could tell his wife was heating up. He got up from the recliner and walked over to his wife. He took his wife in his arms and kissed her sweetly on the lips.

"I'm looking for both, my love."

****

For the next couple of months, James went about the business of purchasing the shopping center next to the church. The owner was eager to sell the property, but he also wanted top dollar for it. James was more than annoyed that the owner was trying to price gouge for a property that was beyond neglected. Saul had set up an inspection, and the inspector found thousands of dollars' worth of repairs that each separate unit would need before they could remotely start site-specific renovations. The owner wanted to sell the property as-is. James pushed hard to get the owner to make the costly repairs. Finally, James told him it was either make the renovations and get top dollar or take the cost out of the asking price. The owner finally settled on taking the cost out of the price.

That's when James and Saul went into overdrive. It was the beginning of the summer, and James wanted all of the renovations done for back to school time. He wanted to host a haircut drive and give school clothes to underprivileged kids. He also wanted to contact the local schools to set up a fundraiser night at the restaurant where they'd receive 30% of the profits if the people mentioned the school's name while dining. He couldn't do any of that if the renovations weren't done. Saul found an affordable contractor with his own crew, but then he also found cheap day laborers at the local Home Depot to work after hours. What should have taken six months to complete, James and Saul did in two-and-a-half months. And James made sure everything was done up to code and with quality work. He supervised the crews day and night.

Alice was extra supportive and made sure that everything was taken care of at home so that James could be where he needed to be. Although Alice was hyper-sexual, she knew she'd need her sex toys to play husband while James was away. In the back of her mind, she was willing to be patient. This wasn't going to be a life change, but rather a temporary one. In the scope of forever, what was a summer, right? Alice knew that James would be no good to the family if he was constantly worrying about the renovation sites, so it was better for him to be there in body and not annoy her in spirit. It didn't go unnoticed. James loved and appreciated his wife very much. He may not have had much energy to show her, but he constantly told her how much he adored her. That's all that Alice wanted. She was a simple woman. Good sex and insightful conversation was what had kept their marriage going for over a decade. They rarely argued, and Alice was the most understanding woman James knew. He had picked his perfect match, and a summer of strain wasn't going to affect that.

It was the end of the summer, and the shops looked incredible. James made sure everything from the storefront design to the landscaping looked as professional as possible. He wanted the community to patronize his businesses, not just church members. Saul put banners out front with all the upcoming community events. There was going to be a back to school walk for single moms and underprivileged families. The families would start at the beginning of the shopping center at the barbershop or beauty salon for back-to-school haircuts or hairstyles. Next, they would go to the thrift store to pick out three sets of pants and shirts. The church had received tons of clothing donations at the thrift shop, so there was plenty to give away. Next, they would go to the restaurant for lunch. Finally, they would visit the pediatrician who donated her time to do physicals out of the counseling office. There were private offices, so she and the doctors in her practice could give the families privacy during their screenings. James had everything scheduled and ready to go. He was proud of the hard work he'd done and the sacrifices he and his loyal crew made during the summer.

The One and Only Lily

James found himself happier than he'd ever been these days. His membership had grown from 1,000 people to 3,000 in just a few months. The community seemed to rally around his modern style of preaching. He talked about wealth, prosperity, and living in abundance. Gone were the hellfire and brimstone days of preaching. The people wanted to be encouraged, not made to feel bad for being human. James believed every word he said. He wasn't personally a religious man, but he studied his Bible for relevant scriptures every day. He wanted the people to know he was well versed and that his philosophies were backed by the Bible. James loved being in the limelight again. His name was on everyone's lips. He may not have been everyone's pastor, but he definitely attracted a lot of attention. He was, in fact, a handsome celebrity. The women around town always batted their eyes around him. The guys asked for his autograph. They also commented on how lucky he was to be married to Alice. Four kids later, and she was still a fox! She'd bounced back beautifully after having her twin pregnancies. She did have a little pooch leftover after the second set of twins, but not noticeable with her clothes on. This was phenomenal for any mom. Most women would kill for her body, and most men lusted after it. James was indeed a lucky man.

James walked into the counseling office that was serving as a clinic during the church's back-to-school walk. He greeted the pediatrician's nurse at the door and kept walking to the different counseling rooms. Each doctor was staged in a different room and waiting for the kids to arrive. James greeted each doctor who were all on their cell phones either scrolling or talking to someone. In the last room, when James peeked his head in the door, the doctor was on a laptop typing feverously. "Good morning. I don't want to interrupt. I just wanted to say hello." James said with a smile. The doctor looked up.

"Good morning, Pastor James. I'm Lily." She said as she peered over the top of the computer.

"Ah, Lily. Thanks so much for volunteering your practice today. It's not every day that a doctor works on a Saturday." James pushed the door all the way open and stepped inside. He extended his hand to shake Lily's. Lily slid the laptop further back on the desk and stood up. James couldn't see them at first, but her tall legs were tucked tightly underneath the table. So, when she stood, all six feet of her were basically looking James eye to eye. She extended her hand and met James' in the middle of the desk.

"It's my pleasure. Our kids are so special, so it's the least I could do. Once this is over, I'd love to talk to you about providing health screenings through the church. Early detection of certain health conditions could help us extend the lives of our community members. Can I set up a meeting through your office?" James studied Lily for a moment. He was taken aback from the moment she stood up. Lily was tall, tan, and had beautiful jet black hair. Her facial features were unique. Take each part away, and she wasn't so attractive. But altogether, it somehow made her exotic and gorgeous. Her tall frame was slim yet curvy. Her breasts were perky and noticeable through a conservative blouse underneath her lab jacket. Although she was fully clothed, James could tell she exercised regularly and was in great physical shape. And he was *impressed*. She was a doctor, for precious children no less, and a community servant. What wasn't attractive about Lily? James realized he was holding Lily's hand too long when she pulled it away. He also realized he didn't answer her question.

"Yes. Of course. My assistant will be happy to schedule something." James flashed her a million dollar smile.

"Wow, you *are* as handsome as they say." James blushed. Lily realized she may have spoken out of turn, so she quickly turned away, found the chair behind the desk, and sat in it. She pulled the laptop closer to her. She looked back up at James who was giving her a "it's ok" look. "Forgive me for being inappropriate." Lily said with embarrassment.

"It's ok, Lily. It was a pleasure to meet you, and I look forward to meeting with you about the health screenings soon. I think it's needed, and I'm only sorry I didn't think about it first." James turned to walk out of the room but stopped quickly. He turned back to see that Lily had started typing again on the computer. "Hey, Dr. Lily. Are you a member of my church?" Lily peered over the laptop.

"No sir. I've been to a couple of services, but I haven't decided if I want to join or not."

"That's a shame. Here, I'll make you a bet." Lily interrupted.

"Do pastors make bets?"

"This one does." James answered. "Do you like sports?"

"Yes." Lily replied.

"Do you follow football?" Lily smiled before she answered.

"I'm the Panthers' number one fan."

"Great. I'll make you a bet, Panthers fan. If the Panthers lose to the Bills in tomorrow's preseason game, then you have to get off the fence and join the church. Deal?"

"I'm not sure how that's a deal, but I'll take those odds. I believe in my team's abilities. We look good so far, so I'll take my chances." Lily stood up again and extended her arm to shake James' hand on their deal. James walked back over to Lily and firmly shook her hand. He looked into her eyes that were beaming with pride. She was confident. Sure of the deal she was making. That caught James off guard, because he hadn't seen that kind of confidence in a woman since he'd met Alice. It was rare for a woman to catch James' eye, but Lily was definitely someone special. James could feel the trouble stirring in his stomach as he turned and walked out of the office and closed the door. He walked down the hallway and passed the closed doors. He could hear the families arriving in the lobby, and that's the only thing that snapped him out of the stupor he'd gotten into while thinking of Lily. He didn't know if she'd be good or bad trouble, but he didn't have time to think about it. It was time for him to get into pastor-mode and greet the families along the back-to-school walk.

James found himself avoiding the counseling center. He didn't want to run into Lily again. She had obviously piqued his interest, but he was a happily married man. Anything more with Lily would have been unprofessional and ill-advised. Avoiding the counseling center seemed like the best course of action. James greeted every family. There was a table by the coin laundry that Saul and Alice were tending too. James looked down the sidewalk and Alice was laughing at something Saul was saying. It was the reminder he needed that Alice was the love of his life. All other women paled in comparison to her beauty, her grace, her style, and the amazing sexual connection they've always had. She was his match in every way. James made his way down the sidewalk to Alice and Saul. As he approached, Alice saw him coming and motioned for him to come closer.

"Listen to this, babe." Alice looked at Saul. "Tell James the story." Alice started laughing again. "This is killing me. Tell him, tell him!" James started to chuckle because Alice was so tickled by something. He looked at Saul who was a little embarrassed at all the fuss Alice was making.

Saul began. "So, you remember how the contractor told us how they'd be delayed and would need more time?" James nodded in agreement. "Ok, well, I was telling Alice the story about how we picked up the crew to come in at night to make up the time difference." James nodded again, but he was waiting for the funny part. He looked at Saul with a face of *and then...* Saul continued. "So one night, before the crew and I got there, the contractor decided to bring his mistress to the site to show it off to her. She was a hairdresser, and we were, essentially, building her dream salon. He was all proud of his work, which was basically our work, and trying to get lucky. She was impressed and wanted to show her gratitude for him bringing her there. So, she drops to her knees, unbuckles his pants, and BOOM! His wife walks in. She must have followed him to the site not believing he was working nights there like he said he was. Me and the crew walked up to see the wife whoopin' her tale, still on her knees mind you, and the contractor trying to button up his pants to stop his girlfriend's beating." Alice interrupted.

"But that's not the best part. Tell him the best part."

Saul motioned for her to slow down. "I was getting there." He turned to James. "The best part was, this was her hairdresser. The contractor was sleeping with his wife's actual hairdresser. She was pissed at him and the girl, and yelled, 'Now I have to go to one of these other bums because you're f-ing the best one!'

48

She was pissed he messed up her hair connection. Not that he was cheating, but that he messed with her hair. Me and the crew were standing there, dying laughing. The three of them ran out of there like bats out of heck. The next morning, the contractor showed up on time, pushed his crew hard, and NEVER mentioned being delayed again." James' jaw dropped while Saul was telling the story. He'd never heard this story before.

"That's hilarious! Why didn't you ever tell me that story?" Saul stopped smiling and looked in the air for an answer.

"I don't know. It was so funny to me at the time, and I can't remember why I didn't tell you. I'm sorry, pastor. It's not like me to forget something like that." Saul began to apologize emphatically. James patted him on the shoulder to let him know it was ok.

"Hey man, I'm not coming down on you. Relax!" James reached out and patted Saul on the shoulder again. "How are we doing on bookbags? Do we have enough to finish out the drive?" James asked. Alice answered.

"We have plenty. Actually, I think we're going to have enough to send with the doctor back to her practice. I'm sure there were some families that couldn't make it today that she'll see before we do." James hadn't thought about Lily in a while. She was out of sight, but Alice's idea just brought the thought of Lily's perky breasts and tall frame back to James' mind. James had to shake off the thought.

"That's a great idea, honey. Why don't you go ahead and pack them up now. I'll let the assistant know the plan." James turned from the table and headed towards the counseling office. The last families were leaving, and the doctors had gathered at the reception area. Everyone was there but Lily. James excused his way through the families and the doctors to the receptionist. "Hello there. How'd it go today?"

"It was great! We saw a lot of kids, and I think we earned a few new patients, too." Said the receptionist.

"That's good to hear. Say, do you think y'all could find some families to give away the last of the bookbags. We have some leftovers, and we want to put every bookbag in the hands of the kids who need them." James heard a voice answer him over his shoulder.

"Of course we can." James turned to find Lily standing behind him. She had her lab coat draped over her left forearm and her large purse hanging over her right shoulder. Her hands were clasped in front of her, but her stance was very model-esque. Now James could see her entire frame and that Lily's pants were fitted to the hips to expose her hourglass shape. He let his eyes glance over her very obviously. He couldn't hide the fact that he found her attractive. It wasn't normal for James to feel an attraction to anyone other than Alice, so he honestly didn't know how to act. It took Lily's blush to break James's glaze.

"That's great. My beautiful wife, Alice, is packing them up right now." There! James felt a little better that he mentioned his matrimony out loud. Maybe this would shake him out of the embarrassing moment where he let a woman see his thirst. "I'll have her bring them in here to you." James continued.

"No, I'm headed out now. I'll walk out there with you and put them in my trunk while I'm thinking about it." Lily unclasped her hands and extended her hand to James as if to say *after you*. James couldn't find the strength to refuse, so he walked towards the door and pushed it open to hold it for Lily to pass. "Such a gentleman." Lily remarked, as she walked out of the open door. James looked down and saw the swagger in her bottom. He took notice of her entire frame, and her butt sat high and tight. Its round shape made James think that she was either wearing those booty popping underwear, or there was a natural perfection to that ass. Either way, James had to avert his gaze to avoid the sight of it because he could feel his blood pressure and *nature* start to rise. When he turned to the direction of Alice, he saw that she was just closing the large box with the bookbags packed. Saul was standing there and saw Lily and James approach.

"Good after…" Saul cleared his throat and started over with a deeper voice. "Good afternoon, doctor. How'd it go in there today?" He asked sincerely. Saul wasn't the most attractive man. He was about average height for a man, but he had kept up his workout routine from his military days. What Saul lacked in looks, he more than made up for it in sex appeal. Lily smiled and answered.

"Hey Saul. Thanks so much for setting this up. We had a blast today. The kids were so cute, and thank God, all healthy." Lily walked over and hugged Saul across the table. Alice wasn't truly aware of Lily's presence. She finished up with the box before she actually took the time to study the extreme beauty that was before her.

"Oh wow, you're gorgeous! James, isn't she gorgeous." Alice looked to James for confirmation.

"The only beauty I see is yours, my love." James answered boastfully. Sure, he was trying to garner points from his wife, but he also didn't want to let on the fact that he'd been lusting over Lily's body just moments earlier.

"Oh don't play like you don't have eyes, James. This is a fantastic specimen before us!" Lily's face became completely flushed.

"Thank you, ma'am. That means a lot coming from you. I've followed your entire career all the way to your last Olympics before retirement. And, I must say, I aspired to be like you, although I never made it past undergrad. It became too much to balance sports and medical school. I had to choose. I chose medicine." Lily shrugged.

"Ahhh, a fellow volleyball player? Do you still play?" Alice inquired.

"No ma'am." Answered Lily. "Every once in a while, I'll join an old lady league just to get back in shape or if a friend asks, but I'm far too busy these days to pursue it more than occasionally." Alice couldn't help but be impressed by her counterpart. She was beautiful, an athlete, and a successful doctor. Alice never found herself to feel jealous, so that wasn't what she was experiencing at the moment. She studied Lily's face and her unique features. She looked at her body and all its perfection. The feeling that she garnered was pride. She was proud of a fellow volleyball player who found her way in the world outside of sports, and it seemed like she was doing all right. Alice noticed the lack of a wedding ring on her finger.

"And a single gal, I see. Saul, why don't you close your mouth and help the good doctor take this box to her car." Alice didn't bother to take her eyes off of Lily, but she could tell by his entire posture that Saul was thoroughly enjoying the view before him. Saul grabbed the box from in front of Alice and slid it down the table to the end towards the parking lot. When he got to the end of the table, he motioned for Lily.

"Lead the way, good doctor." Saul said with a spirit of servitude. Lily retrieved the keys from her purse and used the fob to open the trunk of her late model, luxury electric SUV. Saul saw the trunk open and made his way to the vehicle. Lily took a few steps and turned back to address Alice one last time.

"It was a pleasure to finally meet you, First Lady." Lily said with a smile.

"Please, call me Alice." Alice replied.

"Alice." Lily whispered. "What an honor. Thank you. I'll see you in service tomorrow." Alice nodded humbly and with a smile. Lily then turned to James. "And I'll see you at some point during the week for our meeting. I think we can really positively impact the health of this community. Really prolong lives. I'll draw up some ideas and contact your secretary.

James replied. "Sounds good. Thanks again doc." James could feel his wife's eyes turn to him when Lily said they would have an appointment. James turned to his wife and said. "Alice and I will be there." He wanted to flash her a look that sent a wave of security her way. To let her know that he only had eyes for her, and it worked. Alice's surprised face relaxed into a loving smile. James made it a point not to look back in Lily's direction, but he listened as she and Saul stood at the rear of her vehicle.

"Do you mind if I call you this week? I'd love to take you to dinner to show my appreciation for your generosity today." Saul said as he looked up into Lily's almond-shaped eyes.

"That sounds fantastic, Saul. Give me a call mid-week, and we'll set something up." Lily said as she broke his gaze. She then walked around to the driver's side door and quickly opened it and hopped in without another word. Lily pulled off quickly, making dirt smoke cloud the air around Saul. Saul walked back towards James, shaking his raised fist back and forth vigorously in victory. He walked right up to James to give him a high-five, in which James shook his head to negate the gesture.

"Oh you're going to leave me hangin'?" Saul asked. James nodded his head yes. "Really pastor? My first date in two years, and you're not happy for me?" Saul asked, looking for an answer.

"It's not that I'm not happy for you, Saul. I just don't objectify women like that." James responded.

"Oh can it, James! That woman was a flat out 10, and you know it! Give that man a high-five." Alice demanded. James put up his hand and slapped Saul's hand with a loud clap. He looked Saul in the eyes and mouthed the words "my man" inaudibly. Saul beamed with pride.

James had never watched a football game so intently. The Panthers weren't his team, so he had no problem cheering against them so fervently. It was the fourth quarter, at the end of the two-minute warning. The Panthers were up by 3, but the Bills had the ball on their 40-yard line. The center snapped the ball. It was a run that only gained three yards. Neither team had a timeout left, so the Bills' quarterback hurried to the line again. "A run? That's a terrible play call with no timeouts." James said aloud to himself. The guys get to the line again. The center snaps the ball, but the quarterback bobbles the snap. He laid down immediately. A loss of two. Now, it was the third down with nine yards to go. Time has ticked down to 00:51 seconds. The Bills lined up, and there was a quick snap. The quarterback dropped back, spotted his target, who had just put a heck of a move on the defender, running down the right sideline. He drew back and let the ball fly. It soared through the air with a perfect spiral. The safety was nowhere to be found, and the Bills receiver caught the ball, in stride, over his shoulder. 12 yards later, and the Bills were up by 3, with only 29 seconds to go. The extra point was good, and it would take an act of God for the Panthers to drive down the field with so little time and so little weapons to combat the Bills defense. Time ran out, and the Bills had won. James celebrated the win bodaciously and thought of his ability to gloat when he saw Lily.

Alice entered the room silently. She walked over to James, who had been standing up cheering at the television while watching the football game. She gave him a kiss on the lips, and intended to walk past him, but James grabbed her by the waist. He turned her body towards his and drew her closer to give her a deep, mouth-watering kiss. Alice pulled her body in closer to James to press her pelvis against his. She could feel that he was already excited. Football had never gotten James excited like this, but Alice liked whatever it was that had gotten into him.

James lifted Alice off of her feet. She wrapped her legs around his waist as he continued to kiss her passionately as he carried her through the living room, down the hallway, and up the stairs. He used his foot to kick their bedroom door open and walked through the door. Alice reached up her hand, grabbed the door and flung it hard so it would shut. Alice was waiting for her husband to stop at the bed, but he kept walking into the bathroom. They stopped kissing as James sat Alice on the dual vanity sink and began to rip her clothes off forcefully. Alice was shocked and delighted. She moaned as James' hands raced across her skin and tugged at her clothes. She wanted to help James undress, but he pushed her hands away. Once she was naked, James took a step back to admire the virtue of her womanhood. He then turned and walked to the shower. He grabbed the handle and turned on the rain shower to the hottest setting, generating steam. He then turned back to Alice. He locked eyes with her as he pulled his shirt over his head. Alice watched with lust in her eyes as James pulled down his basketball shorts and boxer briefs. James kicked his shorts and underwear towards Alice as an invitation to meet her naked form. Alice walked over to him and pushed him with both hands on the chest. James stumbled back a few steps, but Alice quickly approached him to make up the space between them. She then pushed him again forcefully, to which made him stumble backwards again. James realized she was pushing him towards the shower, so he turned and stepped over the threshold of the glass shower and onto the tile shower floor. Alice was quickly behind him. Both James and Alice walked under the rain shower, completely soaking their naked bodies and making them glisten. James grabbed Alice by the waist and spun her around. He kissed the back of her neck as he ran his hand around to her stomach and let his hands run up her body to lead towards her breasts. He caressed her breasts and pulled them upward and outward, squeezing gently. He then lightly pinched her nipples, sending shockwaves to Alice's clitoris. James took one hand and ran it up to lightly squeeze Alice's neck as he continued to kiss her back, neck, and ears. He ran the other hand down to her vagina to please her manually. James drew back his hand quickly when he felt how turned on Alice was. Her sticky goodness was too slippery for him to get a good feeling of where

Alice's love button was, so he used his pelvis to walk her body forward towards the shower wall. Alice put her hands out to brace herself into position. James grabbed his loaded gun and pushed it hard into Alice. She groaned with pleasure as he drew back, withdrawing his love. He then put his hands on the small of Alice's back, using his thumbs to push an arch in her back. Alice braced herself again as James thrust his manhood into her again. James growled with pleasure as Alice's moisture wrapped around him like a gloved hand. James had never felt so excited. He wanted to please his wife, but he also wanted to satisfy the urgency in his stroke. James knew he needed to slow down. He slowed his pace, slowed his stroke, and took a deep breath. Alice was having no parts of the slow speed. She pushed her butt back on James with force. "If you're going to fuck me, fuck me." Alice announced. James was shocked. He hadn't realized that his wife was looking forward to the rough part of sex. His demeanor was forceful at first, so it was only natural for Alice to want James to continue the intensity. James took the challenge and long-stroked his wife like a porn star. He pulled back as far as he could without falling out and thrusted forward and upward for max impact. Normally, Alice would reserve her screams for when the children weren't home, but she could contain herself. James was giving her every inch of him, and it was thrilling to her. He could feel her body start to tremble in anticipation of her climax. James knew it was a great time for him to lose focus and climax with her. He squeezed Alice's waist tightly, took one step closer to gain his footing, and reached around to manually stimulate Alice into ecstasy as he found his climax too. James unloaded with fury as he shut his eyes tightly, tilted his head up, and growled with pleasure. He stepped back into the rainfall and opened his eyes. He saw Lily staring back at him in delight. James blinked quickly and rubbed his eyes.

"Are you ok, babe?" Alice asked as she approached James at the rainfall.

"Yeah, I'm fine. Um. Just a little water in my eyes." James lied. "Round two?" James asked as he wrapped his arms around Alice's shoulders and pulled her closer to kiss her sweetly on the lips.

"As good as that sounds, I have to get the boys ready for school tomorrow. Now that we lose part of our Sundays for service, I end up starting prep for the week a little later. Rain check?" Alice asked as she wiggled her way out of James' grip and reached for the soap in the set-in dish behind him.

"Rain check." James responded as he reached past Alice to get his body wash dispenser from the standing shower caddy.

The Impulse

James looked forward to his meeting with Lily all week. She scheduled the meeting for Thursday afternoon. James looked for her in Wednesday's Bible study, but Lily wasn't there. Finally, Thursday morning had arrived, and James put on a tight fitting white t-shirt under his blazer and some fitted jeans. He wanted Lily to be excited by his physical appearance. He knew there would never be a world where the two of them could be together, but he wanted Lily to desire to be with him. He had lusted over her in the counseling office and even envisioned her in his moment of ecstasy in the shower with Alice, but he had no clue if Lily had the same feelings. James dressed with purpose. Although his appearance to the naked eye was a plain t-shirt and jeans, James knew how to enhance his features that were most attractive. He'd watched the women in town; they would always stare at his bulging muscular arms and chest. He also knew they loved his sultry, deep voice. James would use those assets to his advantage later in the afternoon when he saw Lily.

It wasn't always that James found himself distracted. He usually prided himself on his laser focus and determination to make everyday a great day. But today was different. Today he felt butterflies in his stomach. It was almost like the anticipation he felt for his first date with Alice. James never thought another woman could make him feel this way, especially because he was a happily married man. Alice was perfect in every way, so how could James be so nervous about meeting with another woman? James tried to distract himself. He looked for scriptures in the Bible to go along with his sermon, but that didn't take long enough. He walked over to the church businesses next door to check on them, but business was booming. The parking lot was full, and each business was far too busy to stop and chat with him, so James made his way back into his church office. Finally, James decided to leave and go for a drive to clear his mind. Driving always made him feel better. James set himself an alarm on his cell phone for 2:30 p.m. That way, he could start making his way back to the church to arrive in time for his 3:00 p.m. meeting with Lily.

Just as he'd anticipated, the drive helped James put his life back into perspective. It wasn't often that a woman impressed him. In college and in his pro days, he had seen plenty of beautiful women hanging outside of his hotel room or at parties. He needed more than a pretty face and a desirable body to really catch his attention. And yes, Lily was *impressive*, but she wasn't Alice. Not by a longshot. She wasn't the doting mother to his four sons. She wasn't the woman who supported him in a career change or a move clear across the country, and she wasn't the woman that continued to surprise him in the bedroom. Alice's *fuck me* demand was strange, but exciting. She'd talked dirty to him before, but she was never so forceful and demanding with it. That was so like Alice. Full of surprises even after so many years of marriage.

James pulled back into his reserved space at exactly 3:00 p.m. He saw Lily's car farther into the parking lot. He felt badly that the time had gotten away from him. He hated to be late, even if it was just by a minute. He trotted up the back stairway that led to the offices. James took a few steps towards his office. He could see Saul sitting at his secretary's desk, but when he glanced to the left, all he could see were black stiletto heels. *Oh no*, James thought as he continued to walk forward. *Not heels*. With each step another part of the masterpiece that is Lily was revealed. Her long legs were covered by her jeans, but it seemed like the jean material went on forever. James looked over at Saul who hadn't even noticed he'd walked into the door. He couldn't take his eyes off of Lily either. James walked closer to see all of Lily. She had on a green blouse with white flowers that was low cut at the breast. James realized that the drive had only momentarily cleared his mind. Seeing Lily brought him right back into the same cloudy head space. She looked so beautiful, and James couldn't help but admire her from his safe distance. Saul finally looked his way.

"Oh, Pastor! We didn't hear you come in." James chuckled a little. Saul was using "we" terms. It made James laugh because Saul hadn't known this woman but a week, yet he was already claiming her as his other half.

"Good afternoon, good people." James said in his extra deep voice. "Saul, I wasn't expecting to see you today." James looked at Saul who was grinning ear to ear.

"I have the pleasure of escorting this beautiful lady to an early dinner after your meeting today. It's her birthday." Saul extended his arm in Lily's direction with an open palm. He continued. "I figured I could wait while y'all meet, and we could just leave from here." James looked at Lily, who was smiling without any teeth.

"It's been a while since I've been on a date." Lily began. "I'm usually too busy. But an early dinner works out for me right now, so what the heck. Let go and let God, right?" James could tell that Lily wasn't interested in Saul. She was just being kind.

"Well, don't let me slow down a love connection or the birthday celebration. Why don't you guys go ahead now, and I'll catch up with you some other time." James asked, knowing the answer.

"No!" Lily insisted. "I don't have any other openings until about two weeks from now. And who knows what your schedule looks like. Let's just meet quickly, and Saul and I will be off to dinner before we know it. Is that ok with you, Saul?" Lily asked as she stood up, already putting her plan into motion.

"Of course." Saul answered immediately. "Pastor, Tina said she was going to get your afternoon refresher tea from the coffee shop. She said she'll be right back, but if you need something else, call her on her cell."

"Thanks, Saul." James replied. "I was wondering where she'd gone. She knew I had a 3 o'clock on the books, so she'll probably stop and get her nails done before I ever see that refresher." The trio all laughed to themselves. "Right this way, Lily. Saul, we'll make it quick. Do you know where you're taking this lovely lady yet?" James inquired. Saul gave an all teeth smile.

"The Homestyle Buffet." Saul said with pride. James busted out laughing, but Lily wasn't amused. She rolled her eyes and turned towards James' office. "Wait, I'm joking." Saul called after her. Lily pushed the door to the office open and walked in.

She went and sat down on the chair closest to the door and crossed her legs. James looked at Saul with a face of sympathy, as if he'd just messed up royally. Saul gave himself a fake punch in the nose. James walked into his office. Saul called into the closing door. "I'll be right here when you're done." Then James closed the door.

He made it a point to look up as he walked around Lily to the other side of the desk. He also made it a point to look down at the paperwork on his desk so as to not admire Lily as he sat down. James closed his eyes, and only opened them when he knew his gaze was positioned exactly on Lily's face. Lily was smiling, but she wasn't looking at James. She was looking around the room. James assumed she was admiring all the trophies and pictures he had scattered around the room. His office was, in part, a shrine to his accomplishments. He finally spoke to get Lily to refocus on his eyes. "Impressive, huh?" James asked.

"What?" Lily asked puzzled.

"The room. This office was designed by a professional when I first moved into this building."

"Oh yes. It is lovely." Lily said hurriedly. "No, I was actually looking for artwork. I'm an art collector in my not so free time. I always like to scan new surroundings for unique art pieces." James felt embarrassed. Here he was thinking he'd impressed Lily with his ode to himself, but she hadn't even noticed. Just like she didn't notice his carefully put together outfit. James started to realize that Lily wasn't like the other women in town. She wasn't excited about his status or wealth. She remarked about his handsomeness before, but she hadn't noticed how well-groomed he was today, and she wasn't impressed by his office. Why she wasn't throwing herself at his feet wasn't bothering James as much as why he cared so much that she wasn't.

"So what brings you here today, doctor? What can the Bread of Life do to help you reach more people in the community?" James leaned back in his chair and crossed his arms over his chest as he listened. Lily began.

"I believe we have too many children in this community that aren't immunized or properly trained in how food nutrition plays a huge role in healthier lifestyles well into their teenage years and adulthood. What I'm proposing is my practice partner up with the church to hold free after school care for the youth in this area. It gives parents a free and safe place to send their kids after school that will focus on mind, body, and spirit. Imagine spending the first half hour gathering the kids and providing them with a healthy snack. Then, we can spend the next hour working on homework and tutoring for those who need it. We could use the next hour to focus on health and fitness. If you remember, when we were kids, our parents used to make us finish our homework and then go outside and play. We would play outside for hours and weren't allowed to come back inside until it was time for dinner. With the dawning of the digital age, our kids are addicted to screens and don't want to play outside anymore. Changing ways calls for changing plays." Lily lightly smirked at her play on words, then continued.

"Finally, we can feed the children a healthy meal and provide health screenings for the last hour. They can also have free play until their parents come to sign them out. I think the healthy meal part of it is the most important to me. Our children eat a Mc-something or another every night, or those instant noodles which leads to childhood obesity and, even worse, health problems into adulthood. You have a perfectly functional kitchen in the fellowship hall. Why don't we put that to good use. If you're interested, I can set up this program with volunteers from the church community. I have a girlfriend who runs a grant-funded supper program. She can provide the free meals. We can ask church members to volunteer as tutors and program monitors. I'll get the doctors from my practice to volunteer one day a week, so all five days are covered for health screenings. All you'll need to do is provide the building and designate a place in the event hall for the program. What do you think?" James uncrossed his arms and leaned forward to respond.

"It seems like you've already planned this out. Do you really need me?" James asked with a laugh.

"I've had this idea for a while, but I didn't have a location with the space to accommodate a large amount of children." Lily was laser-focused. She didn't crack a single smile. She was all business. James could tell she was passionate about what she was saying, and her plan was well thought out. He couldn't think of a reason why the program wouldn't work. He could feel her heart was beating for this, and he wanted to make her heart happy. James wondered why he was feeling the need to make her happy. He'd looked forward to their meeting since the Panthers lost, and he hadn't even had a chance to tease Lily about it. Lily was on a mission and wasn't having any other distractions curve the conversation.

"Listen, I love the idea. I think it's great. My only concern is going too big too fast. Let's start with 50 students and see where it goes. If we're going to rely on volunteers, then we'll need to make sure we have enough eyes around for proper supervision." Lily finally cracked a smile.

"Sure, Pastor. That sounds like a plan."

James stood up and walked around the desk towards Lily. Lily stood too. James opened his arms wide to embrace Lily as a form of solidifying their new contract. Lily walked right into James' chest and wrapped her arms around his waist. James wrapped his arms around Lily's shoulders and hugged her body tight. Then Lily did something James didn't expect. She laid her head on his chest and inhaled deeply as if she were taking in his essence. It finally hit him that Lily was trying to keep herself composed just as he had been doing. James released Lily from his tight grip and looked at her face from his close view. Her eyes had a look of gratitude and a hint of innocence. He felt a deep connection while looking into her eyes. There was obviously an attraction between the two, and James couldn't help himself. He grabbed Lily's face by the chin, tilted it up towards his, and laid the sweetest kiss on her lips. Lily wrapped her arms around James' neck and pulled him forward to press her lips into his for a deeper kiss. James felt her mouth open, so he responded by lightly running his tongue across the inside of her mouth. Her breath was warm and inviting. Lily ran her hands into James' hair and pressed her breasts against James' chest drawing him in and inviting him to continue. As he felt her breasts, James could also feel his manhood rise. That's when he finally snapped back into reality. He was kissing a woman that wasn't his wife. He even thought to himself, *Oh shit! I'm kissing a woman that isn't my wife.*

James stepped back abruptly and ran into the front of his desk, knocking over the pencil holder. He ran his middle three fingers across his lips and looked at the pink lipstick that had collected on his lips from the kiss with Lily. James was in full shock. He hadn't expected to kiss her, but he couldn't resist the impulse to be close to her. There was something about Lily that made James feel like it was ok, but he had no clue what was happening. She didn't stop him, either. It felt like she was inviting him to more. But James was confused and trying to catch his bearings. Lily took a step closer to him and into his awkward gaze. James looked into Lily's eyes which were telling him she was ok. She was giving him permission to continue if he wanted to or stop if he wasn't comfortable. Who was this woman? How could she be reading his mind? How did she know just the right look to give him in that moment to set him at ease? James half smiled and returned his gaze to the floor.

Lily could tell James was uncomfortable. She adjusted herself and her clothes then took a compact out of her purse to check her lipstick. She used the powder muff to remove the lipstick from around her lip line where James' lips landed just outside of hers. She then pulled out a lipstick to reapply. James looked up at Lily, and suddenly he grabbed the lipstick out of her hand. He closed it and dropped it on the floor. He grabbed Lily by the shoulders and drew her closer to kiss her again, but he didn't go for her lips this time, he planted his passionate kiss on her neck. Lily drew in a deep breath through her nose and slowly exhaled through her mouth so as to not make a sound that could be heard from outside of the room. James then kissed down the front of her body as he pulled her breast out from her bra and exposed it through the V in her green, flower shirt. Lily let out a tiny gasp and James feverishly licked and sucked on her breast. Lily gave into James as he grabbed her by the waistline of her jeans. He unzipped her pants and pulled them down along with her lacy, green panties as he dropped to his knees. He then turned Lily to put her back to the desk and gently pressed her backwards until her buttocks rested on the top of his desk with the sound of a small bump. Lily must have known what was coming next because she slightly opened her legs to allow James to put his entire face and tongue against her button. James unleashed his tongue and unhinged his jaw to give Lily heights of pleasure she hadn't had in a while. It didn't take long for Lily to feel the warm chills tingling her body in anticipation of the inevitable starburst that rushed her internal walls. She could feel intense sensations flowing through her full being from her hair follicles to the cuticles on her toes. Lily internally enjoyed the experience too, knowing that Saul and the secretary were merely a few feet outside of the door.

James sat back on his bottom to relieve his knees. With his feet on the floor, he pulled his knees towards his chest and wrapped his arms around them to clasp his hands together. James couldn't believe what just happened. To him, it was the kind of thing that you only see in movies. It was an outer body experience. Never in a million years would he have imagined that he would be so excited by a woman that he would kiss her, let alone perform mouth love on her. Lily pulled up her panties and then her jeans. She buttoned her pants and adjusted her clothing again. She searched the floor for her compact and lipstick that were flung in two different directions. Lily then went about the business of fixing her face again. No words were exchanged between James and Lily. They both were fully aware of what just happened, but there wasn't any need for words. They both needed time to process the delightfully dirty deed that just transpired. Lily finished her face and walked towards James who was still hugging his knees. She kissed him on the top of his head sweetly. James unclasped his hands and used a nearby chair to stand up. He adjusted the furniture back to its original spot and reorganized his desk that had been used as a prop in his lovefest. Lily waited for James to calm down and turn to face her. When James did, Lily took the time to adjust his clothing back into place. She grabbed a tissue from the box on his desk to wipe the lipstick and the product of her excitement from his face. She then went into her purse and pulled out a pack of gum. She pulled out a piece, unwrapped it, and pushed it directly into James' mouth. James found himself in total shock.

"How are you so calm right now?" He asked with a puzzled look on his face.

"I'm a doctor. I'm always calm under pressure. I'm also great at keeping confidential records." Lily said with a wink. James smiled in relief. Lily continued. "Listen, neither one of us was expecting that, right? You didn't plan that, did you?" James' eyes got wide, and he quickly answered.

"No! That was pure impulse." He put his hands up in a defensive posture.

"See! This was a one-time act of randomness that caught us both off guard. Now that it's happened, we can be more intentional that it won't happen again. Now put that thing away…" Lily motioned her hand down towards James' erection. "…and we can get out of here and act like nothing ever happened." James quickly adjusted himself and took a few deep breaths.

"I think I'm going to need a little more time. Why don't you go ahead out. See my secretary to schedule our next appointment. Ask her to reach out to our youth minister and our volunteer coordinator to chaperone, I mean attend, our next meeting. We can coordinate a little better if we can stay focused." They both laughed. James walked over and kissed her on the cheek. Lily smiled and turned towards the door. She adjusted her clothing one more time and then turned the handle to open the door. She walked out as if nothing had happened and walked straight to the secretary to follow orders. James peeked behind her as she walked down the hallway. He saw Saul pop up from his seat and throw the magazine he'd been reading back onto the table in a hurry.

James closed the office door and leaned his back on it. He could still smell Lily's sweet nectar in his nose. He could still taste her on his tongue. He basked in her essence for a moment. Knowing that was the first and last time he'd touch her like that was a moment to pause and revel in, and James intended to take that moment. He then walked into his office bathroom and flipped on the light. James was immediately greeted by his reflection in the bathroom mirror. He studied his face for a while. He looked like the same person he'd always been, but who was this person looking back at him right now? Although he didn't actually penetrate this woman with his penis, he had just cheated on his wife. "Where did that come from?" James said aloud. James located the trash and spit out the gum Lily had given him. He turned on the hot water handle and let the water run for a second. When he saw the steam come up from the sink, he turned on the cold water handle slightly to add a manageable amount of cold to cool the hot. He then cupped both hands under the water to collect a pool and leaned forward to splash the water in his face. He cupped his hands to collect more water and sucked the water into his mouth and swirled it around before spitting it out. He repeated the process of splashing his face and swishing his mouth out twice before grabbing the hand towel hanging on the rack to his right and wiping his face. James stood up straight and looked at himself in the mirror again. Talking to himself aloud, James said "Dude, that was a one-time-deal. You can't do that again. You're not going to blow up your entire life for a woman you just met who you happen to be attracted to." James looked down to address his crotch. "And you sir, don't get a say in any of this." James realized his erection was gone. He went to urinate and wash his hands. He felt confident with his pep talk to himself and his johnson. He walked out of the office and down the hall to his secretary. "Hey there. Were you able to get the doctor and our team scheduled for our planning meeting?"

She looked up with a half-smile and replied. "The only day and time you were all available is tomorrow at 4:30 p.m. Is that ok or do you want me to call them back and reschedule for some time next week?" James had to think about it. He thought he would've had some time in between to recover, but he couldn't let on that something was going on.

"Yes, of course. I'll let Alice know when I get home. Tomorrow is our date night, but I'll tell her I'm going to be a little late." James looked down at the calendar on the secretary's desk. He saw Lily's name and phone number written down under tomorrow's date. He looked back up at the secretary. "I think I'm going to head out now. I'm a little tired, and I think my work here is done for the day." The secretary nodded and smiled humbly.

"Good night, Pastor."

James nodded and walked towards the exit. At the moment, James knew that he had it all under control. He was confident that his pep talk in the bathroom had worked, and that tomorrow's meeting would be a breeze. James walked out of the exit and towards his car. He saw Lily's car was still in the parking lot, but Saul's car was gone. They must have taken Saul's car to eat. James stepped into his car and sat for a moment. He started the engine and put the car into gear. When he looked through the windshield, he saw a note that was left in his wiper blade. He put the car in park, opened the door, and pushed the top half of his body through the door to retrieve the note. There was no *to* or *from*. The note simply said "Thank You" and had the kiss of pink lips at the bottom.

"Oh." James said aloud with a whisper. "Lily."

James drove home in a fog. When he pulled up to his home, he didn't know how he had gotten there. The only explanation for his safe arrival had to be muscle memory. His mind was too far gone for him to have actually focused on the road. His pep talk was completely ruined by the note Lily had left him on the windshield of his car. All he could think about was how he acted so out of character. Sports had taught him discipline and control, but there was nothing disciplined or controlled about the way he acted in his office. Saul and his secretary were a few feet away. What if someone had walked in? Hell, what if Alice would have walked in? They were in a place in their marriage that Alice had stopped knocking on doors over a decade ago. There was no need for privacy when you've seen it all and heard it all in a marriage. James was really in the business of beating himself up when he heard a tap on his window. He had to snap himself back into reality. He looked through the driver's side window towards the sound of the tapping. It was his oldest son, Teeny. "Dad, are you going to take me to practice or is mom?" James hadn't taken his seatbelt off. He looked down and realized that he still had his foot on the brake even though he had taken the car out of gear.

"I'll take you, son." James replied. "Holler up there and tell your mother Imma take you." James needed a minute before he could look at Alice, better yet, before he could let Alice see his guilty face. Teeny followed his father's instructions and trotted back to the house. He yelled through the open door, closed it, and locked it with his key. As he trotted back to the car, he must have realized he'd forgotten something in the house. He turned back to the front door, opened it, and retrieved his gym bag from the floor by the door.

"Can't forget my practice uniform again." Teeny yelled down the path towards the car. He jumped across the path and ran through the grass towards the car. He opened the trunk and put his bag in the back and then climbed into the passenger seat next to his dad. "Ready, ready." Teeny announced. James put the car in reverse and backed out of the driveway. As he drove down the road, he didn't say anything. Teeny glanced in his father's direction and then looked out of the passenger side window. The trees passed in a haze as James sped down the road. It was getting dark, and the colors danced across the evening sky. There was a slight fall breeze in the air, so James rolled down the windows to let it whip around the car. "Dad, are you ok?" Teeny questioned.

"I'm fine, son. Why do you ask?" James looked over at his son to see what expression he had on his face, and it was one of concern. He was genuinely concerned that there was something wrong. "What?" James asked, puzzled.

"It's just, you're really quiet tonight. Usually, when you take me to practice, you have some coaching advice for me, or you want to talk about the birds and the bees. But you're really quiet. And quiet ain't like you." James chuckled to himself.

"So usually I get on your nerves, but today I'm too quiet for your liking?" James chuckled again.

"No, it's not like that." Teeny answered. "But you didn't even say anything when I ran on the grass. Usually, I would have gotten a slap on the back of the head or punch in the arm for that. It's like *Invasion of the Body Snatchers* in here." James gave out a full laugh.

"What do you know about *Invasion of the Body Snatchers*? That movie is before your time. Heck, it's before my time." James and Teeny both had a heartfelt laugh. James put his hand on Teeny's shoulder. "I'm sorry, son. I just have a lot on my mind. I had a meeting at the church today that didn't go as planned, so now I'm trying to wrap my head around what I'm going to do next. It's like when you're in the game and you have to anticipate where the ball is going. If you don't play one step ahead, then the other team'll score. Well today son, I got caught off guard, and the other team scored. I just can't wrap my head around how it happened. But I'll figure it out. I always do."

"I hear you, dad." Teeny's face went from one of concern to one of sympathy. He didn't know exactly what happened in the meeting, but he understood the analogy. James pulled into a parking space at the school and put the car in park.

"Do you want me to hang around?"

"No thank you. Kyle's mom is taking us for pizza after practice. Can I have some money?"

"Money!" James shouted in jest. "Man, I'm broke. You got all my money." Teeny laughed.

"Come on, dad." James pulled out his wallet and handed Teeny a $100 bill. "Wow, a hundred!" Teeny exclaimed as he put the money in his pocket and darted off towards the school.

"Grab your bag, Teeny" James shouted behind him. James pressed the button below the dashboard to open the trunk of the car. Teeny came flying back to grab his bag from the trunk and took off running towards the school again. "And I want my change." James shouted through the open window.

James put the car in reverse and headed towards home. He still had to deal with the inevitable. He would have to go home and face Alice. He didn't want to, but he knew that the truth was going to be the best thing for both of them. It was a short drive home, so James psyched himself up to deal with whatever consequences were awaiting him. As he approached his home, there were several cars that lined the street that weren't there before. Some were parked particularly poorly as the driver didn't get close enough to the curb. "Where did all these cars come from? And who is having a party like this during the week?" James asked himself aloud. He slowly maneuvered his way down the street to his home and noticed all of the lights were on in his house and his driveway was full of cars. To the point where he didn't have a way to get to his garage to park. Then it hit him. "Book club." James announced. It was Alice's night to host the book club. She had mentioned it to him earlier in the day, but he had forgotten after the events of the evening. James pulled down the street and parked his car in front of the neighbor's house. He walked his way back to the house and into the unlocked front door. The living room was alive with female chatter. There was a food station set up on the bar and extra copies of the book were stacked on the table in the entranceway. James made his way through the crowd to find Alice. He knew exactly where to find her. Alice never let anyone sit in her favorite chair in the middle of the room. "Babe, I'm sorry. I forgot about book club. I'll head upstairs and get out of your way." James kissed her on the forehead.

"That's ok, honey. Where did you park? I think the girls blocked the driveway." Alice looked around the room at the plethora of women around.

"I'm down the street. I think I'm going to head up to take a shower and then hit the bed. Do you mind moving my car into the garage when everyone is gone?" James asked with puppy dog eyes.

"Sure babe. No problem. Good night." James gave her one more kiss on the forehead and walked away. He waved at the ladies as they admired him as he walked by. He walked down the hallway and up the stairs. James didn't waste any time. He tore off his clothes, leaving a trail on his way to the bathroom, and turned on the shower. He didn't even wait for the water to warm up. He stuck his head under the running water and pressed his palms against the shower walls. The force of the water felt good on his face. It felt like he was washing away the guilt. James knew he would eventually have to face Alice, but he was actually relieved that tonight wasn't the night.

The Secrets

The next morning, James woke up feeling well-rested. He had gone to bed around 7:00 p.m., and the sun was fully risen by the time he woke up. James stretched his arms towards the top of the headboard and looked over to the clock on his nightstand. It read 7:41a.m. He wasn't always the greatest sleeper, but James managed to get over 12 hours of sleep. That hadn't happened for him since he had gotten blackout drunk in college and woke up in a sorority house on a different campus. James chuckled to himself at the memory of his last sleep episode.

He looked over to see Alice's side of the bed only held her imprint. James turned back to his nightstand to retrieve his cell phone. He had a message from Alice. She said she was going to meet some girlfriends at the outlet mall and check on the church's shops before heading home to meet the boys after school. James sent her a quick message to let her know he was ok with her plan for the day and put his phone back on the dresser. The thought of the previous day only crossed his mind when he realized he wouldn't get a chance to tell Alice about his transgression. James slid to the edge of his bed and put his feet on the floor. He rubbed his head hoping to wipe away the memory for the blur that was his life at the moment.

This was probably the worst thing he could have done after over a decade of marriage and four kids, but James also had to come to terms with the fact that ravishing Lily felt so natural. He needed to talk this out with someone. He grabbed his cell phone again and searched his contacts for Dr. Michaels. He found it quickly, because it was saved to his favorites list, and tapped the phone icon to call out. The phone rang twice before Dr. Michaels himself answered.

"Good morning. This is Dr. Michaels." He answered rhythmically. James laughed into the phone.

"I see you still can't get your daughter's boyfriend to do his job, huh?" James said between laughs.

"Ah, that's a voice I've been waiting to hear. James, my friend, how are you?" Dr. Michaels said, laughing back at James' remark.

"I've been doing well. The church seems to be catching fire, and I honestly can't complain. I don't have that empty feeling I had before. This definitely filled the void."

"I'm glad to hear it, but if everything is going well, then why do I have the pleasure of this call today?" Dr. Michaels sounded concerned as he questioned the motives for James' call.

"What do you mean doc? I can't just call to say thank you?" James quipped.

"Sure, but I'd hate to have to bill you for a full hour for just a thank you." Both guys laughed before James came clean.

"Ok doc, you caught me. I've got a situation that I want to talk to you about. This November will be Alice and my 15 year wedding anniversary. 15 years." James repeated with emphasis. "And I love my wife more than peanut M&Ms and popcorn at a baseball game.

"That's a strange comparison." Dr. Michaels remarked. "But go on." James stood to his feet and began to pace the side of his bed before he continued.

"Let's just say I love her a lot. Anyways, so I've been able to avoid being tempted by other women throughout my entire career, all through 15 years of marriage, and through starting a church with about 75% of the new members being women. But there's this woman, doc, that has me questioning myself. She's beautiful and tremendously sexy, but she's more than that. She's a pediatrician who cares about the community, and she makes me feel like I should care more. She's confident. Confident like Alice when I first met her and fell in love with her." Dr. Michaels interrupted.

"James, I'm not hearing a problem here. There will always be women around you. Some may even tempt you. Is this woman trying to get after you?" Dr. Michaels questioned.

"Well, she's got me acting out of character. Yesterday, we were meeting in my office, just to talk about an after school

72

program she was proposing, and I kissed her. Out of nowhere. Just moved in for a kiss."

"Ah, I see." Dr. Michaels responded in his active listening voice.

"Well, it didn't stop there. I pulled away for a second because I realized I was out of control, but then I lost it again. I put her on my desk, and um… well… put my tongue in places a married man shouldn't." James could hear the hesitation on the other end of the phone. "Doc? You still there?"

"Yes, I'm here." Dr. Michaels responded. "I'm just taking some notes so I can have a clear picture of how to respond to your inevitable question. Go on. I'm listening."

"Ok, that's fine." James said relieved that the doctor wasn't judging him already. "I'm losing it, doc. I know I have to tell my wife, and I just agreed to work with this other woman. I don't know how I'm going to keep the peace." Dr. Michaels responded quickly.

"What do you mean keep the peace? Do you plan to keep both of these women in your life?"

"Well, yes." James answered, questioning himself. "I promised an afterschool program that's going to benefit the kids in the community, and I'm not leaving my wife for her. Why wouldn't I be able to keep them both around?" After saying it out loud, James realized how foolish he sounded. He sat back down on the bed and put his left palm to his forehead. It was obvious to him now that Alice would never let him work with a woman who he cheated with, and Lily would have to disappear from his life. That was a sacrifice he'd have to make to keep the peace with his wife, but that's definitely not what he wanted. If adulthood and pastoring had taught him anything, it was that *want to* is luxury and not a necessity in his life. "Ok, so I just heard it out loud, and that sounds really dumb, huh?" James asked, already knowing the answer.

"It's not dumb. You naturally want to bring things closer to you that make you happy. But here's my question for you. Do you plan to leave your wife to pursue a relationship with this other woman?" James definitively answered.

"NO!"

"Ok, so then there's no need to tell your wife. If this is a one-time-deal, and you don't plan on pursuing a relationship, then why would you blow up Alice's world over a one-time mistake?

Do you think this other woman would tell Alice?" James answered definitively again.

"NO!"

"So then there it is. Normally, I would tell my clients to take accountability for their actions, but in this case, we're talking about scandalizing your wife, your family, your church, and your community. The consequences have real ramifications, and this isn't the time for that in your life. My advice would be different if you were in love. But it sounds like infatuation, and you may have killed your curiosity yesterday. Let's do this. Don't say anything to Alice, for now, and see how things play out in the next month. Call me back next month and update me on how the situation develops." Dr. Michael's was making a lot of sense. James hadn't thought about it that way. He wanted to confess his sins to his wife, but he didn't think about how the news would affect her. The doctor was right. James needed to spare Alice the pain and let Lily live the scandal-free, single life she deserved.

"Thanks doc. I hadn't thought about it like that. Yeah, I'll call you next month, and we'll see how this plays out. I think it'll work out just fine. Hey listen, doc. I'm going to get dressed and head to the church. Thanks for the advice. Send me an invoice to my email. I'll lay it straight today." James stood to his feet again in anticipation to the end of the conversation.

"Sounds good. I would tell you to call back and make an appointment with the knucklehead, but chances are, I'll be the one who answers. So I look forward to your call next month."

"Thanks again, doc. I appreciate you. Talk soon."

"Talk soon." Dr. Michaels repeated as he hung up the phone. James felt a weight lift off of his shoulders. He dreaded the idea of hurting Alice, so it was a relief to keep this all to himself. Plus, he knew he wasn't going to fall in love with Lily. It's like the doctor said, he was infatuated with a new woman. The cars on the auto sales lot always look bright and shiny until you have to make the first payment. James felt like he'd won the lottery, and he was going to take full advantage of that feeling.

James quickly got dressed and headed to the church. He had a full day of meetings, but he also had the meeting with Lily and the church crew later in the afternoon. James relished in the fact that he would be distracted all day. He wouldn't have time to think about how awkward it was going to be knowing that Lily was the other participant in the tryst from the previous day.

James was on his best game. Each meeting went better than the previous one. It was a day of winning and highs for the pastor, but also a personal win. James had to remember why he'd entered into a pastor's life. He was missing something that he'd now found. The wins in the boardroom, the amens in church on Sunday, and the recognition in the community. Everything led back to the rockstar status that James was looking for. He'd be remiss if he didn't give credit to himself studying the Bible and preparing for his sermons. One of his hesitations was that he hadn't felt "the calling," but with all the success he'd had as a pastor, there had to be something divine intervening in this world.

James looked at his smartwatch and saw it was almost 4:00 p.m. He felt a hunger pain in his stomach and realized he hadn't eaten all day. He was in back-to-backs, and his secretary hadn't bothered to schedule his lunch. Since he had a minute, James walked across the street to the restaurant to get a bite to eat. After being inside all morning the sunlight was bright on James' eyes. He held up his hand to shield his eyes from the light. Even though the sun was out, it wasn't particularly warm. Fall was in full effect, and the breeze was starting to cool off the highs of the day. As James put his hand out to pull the restaurant door open, he heard a *toot toot* from a car horn. He turned around to see if someone was summoning him, and it was Lily's car pulling up. James froze in his tracks. He wasn't ready to see Lily yet. He hadn't eaten anything, nor had he prepared his mind to see her so soon. But it seemed like she was eager to see him as she waved her hand rapidly in the windshield. The driver's side door opened, and all six feet of Lily climbed out of the car. She reached back into a compartment underneath the steering wheel and retrieved a small wallet, and then closed the door. Lily was wearing scrubs today, but her body wasn't hidden by the unflattering attire. She approached with a skip and a smile. "Hey Pastor McHandsome. I wasn't expecting you to be over here." Lily said as she opened her arms inviting James in for a hug. James obliged and pulled Lily in close. She smelled sweet. He wasn't anticipating a doctor in scrubs to smell like cherry blossoms.

"Hey. You smell nice. Where are you coming from in scrubs and smelling so good." Lily blushed.

"Oh you like that? It's Love Spell by Victoria Secret. I'm a sucker for inexpensive smell goods." James laughed.

"Can't be mad at that." James remarked.

Lily continued. "I had rounds today at the hospital. I wanted to be prepared in case we needed to go into surgery with one of my patients, but they were all doing well, so I got to do what I love about this job, interact with my patients and their families. Plus, I got to catch up on the hospital gossip." Lily said with a chuckle. James smiled, but his hunger was turning into hanger, so he turned towards the restaurant door in an effort to shuttle Lily in his direction.

"I was headed in here to grab something before our meeting. Care to join me?" Lily smiled a shy smile and nodded yes. James pulled the door open and allowed Lily to pass through first. She walked directly up to the lunch counter and sat on a stool. James followed her loosely as he waved at the staff and some of the patrons. He sat on the stool next to Lily who was already studying the menu. James looked at her lovely profile.

"I'm really hungry." Lily announced. "I forgot to eat lunch today." James raised his eyebrows in surprise. She was just like him. So driven and focused that she didn't stop to take care of her basic needs. That was such a turn on to James. A woman who was constantly on a mission. Never allowing idle time to interfere with her task. It just confirmed what James already felt, pure admiration.

"Me too." James finally answered. "I was in back-to-backs, and just came up for air. I already know what I want, so you can take your time. I get the same thing every time."

"Really? The same thing? There's a whole menu here. You don't like to explore a little?" James leaned back on his stool to create some space so he could look at Lily's whole face. Was she flirting with him or was she really talking about food? James was a little off his game, but he was quite sure that Lily was flirting with him. Lily motioned for the waitress to come over. A young lady wearing a jog suit with an order pad came over. "I'm going to have a Reuben sandwich with fries. Can I also get a side salad with the ranch on the side? Then I'm going to get a peach cobbler to go." Lily grabbed her chin as if she was thinking about ordering something else.

"Is that all, honey?" The waitress asked.

"Well. I was thinking about a milkshake, but I don't know if I need the calories."

"I'll tell you what's good. If you mix the peach cobbler and vanilla ice cream, it makes a delicious shake." Lily looked back at the menu to search for the suggestion.

"That does sound delicious, but I don't see it on the menu."

"That's because it ain't on the menu, darlin'. It's my special creation." Lily smiled with all her teeth and with great excitement.

"Oh yes, I'll take it!" Lily then looked over at James who had a look of surprise on his face. "What?" She asked. "A girl's gotta eat, right?" James chuckled.

"Yeah, a girl's gotta eat. I'm just impressed that you're not a dainty woman. You order what you want even though you preach healthy eating habits. Isn't that a little hypocritical?" Lily closed her menu and handed it to the waitress.

"I preach establishing healthy eating habits in children to avoid long haul, sometimes incurable illnesses. But…" Lily said with emphasis. "I am an adult woman who exercises daily and in perfect health. So I can eat what I want. Thank you very much."

"Ok." James put his hands up in surrender. He looked at the waitress who was clearly annoyed with his judgment of Lily's order.

"You'll have your usual blackened chicken salad, I presume?" The waitress said with an attitude.

"Yes please." James replied with a smile. He didn't have to look at Lily to know she was making fun of him. "Now who's judging?" James laughed. Lily burst into laughter too.

"He'll also have the peach cobbler shake." Lily requested from the waitress. They nodded at each other, and the waitress went about the business of putting in their order and making their shakes. Lily looked at James. "You'll thank me later." James put his hands on the counter and didn't protest. The shake actually sounded really good. He loved peach cobbler, and he loved ice cream. He'd had the combination before. He just didn't think to put it into a shake. The fact that Lily was provoking him to try new things was naturally intriguing to him. What other curiosities lie within this beautiful woman? James' smartwatch dinged. He looked down to see a text message from Saul that gave him a 15 minute warning to the meeting. That reminded James that she'd gone on a date with Saul the night before.

"So, how was your date with Saul last night?" James asked, hoping for a positive reaction. If Lily and Saul hit it off, then it would solidify his need to stay away from Lily. Unfortunately, James didn't get the reaction he wanted. Lily's face turned very serious, very quickly.

"It was borderline terrible!" Lily said with emphasis on the terrible. "He took me to this swanky tapas bar with little plates and loud Spanish music. It was expensive too. I felt bad ordering so many little plates and they didn't even hit the bottom of my stomach. I could tell he was doing math in his head when I ordered the fifth plate and another glass of Spanish wine. I told him I had to go to the restroom, but I really went to the waitress, gave her $75, and asked her to subtract that from the bill before she brought it to us. I don't care about the money." Lily looked at James as her eyes pleaded for him to believe her. "I was annoyed that's what he thought I would like. Like, I'm not a Homestyle Buffet kind of girl. That's for sure. But I'm not a swanky tapas kind of girl either."

"Then what kind of girl are you?" James asked.

"I'm a burger and football kind of girl. I'm like a fast casual, Shake Shack and a beer kind of chick. Of course, I'll do a Del Frisco's every once in a while, but I'm super simple. I don't know. I was just kind of turned off by the whole thing. Either way, at the end of the night, I told him I wasn't looking to get serious with anyone, but I'd love to hang out as friends sometime. I think it hurt his feelings, but I also think he understood." James was disappointed that things didn't work out for Lily and Saul.

"I'm really sorry to hear that. He's a good dude. Been through a lot, but he deserves to be happy." Lily put her hand on James' shoulder and took in a deep breath.

"Yep, he sure does. But er ah, it won't be with me." James chuckled and brushed Lily's hand off his shoulder.

"Fine!" He exclaimed. They exchanged a laugh as the food and milkshakes came to the counter. Lily tore right into half of her sandwich with both hands. She grabbed a French fry from her plate and stuffed it into her already full cheek. James poked around at his salad, but he was truly studying Lily. She was an anomaly. Most women try to hide their hunger around him. Even Alice, who he later found out loved to eat, had a salmon salad on their first date. But Lily was different. She wasn't hiding anything. She was her genuine self from the beginning. Plus, she always found a way to compliment him. Which, let's be honest, men love compliments too. James couldn't help but to lose himself in her presence.

James pushed around the food on his plate a little more, but he had to ask. "Are we ever going to talk about yesterday?" He grabbed his milkshake and took a sip. Lily put her sandwich down and grabbed a napkin from the dispenser to wipe her face. She took a sip of her milkshake and swallowed hard to clear the food in her mouth. She looked around to make sure no one was close enough to hear their conversation.

"Listen, I'm happy to never bring it up again. You're a married pastor and I'm a respected pediatrician. It had no business happening in the first place, so if you want, we can pretend that nothing ever happened and move on to the business of the after school program." That was the answer that James needed to hear. She had something to lose in all of this. Her practice's reputation meant a lot to her, so she wouldn't want a scandal to interfere with her livelihood. James thought for a moment before he responded. He leaned in with a whisper.

"I don't know what it is about you that is driving me insane. I don't cheat on my wife. Like, never. But being around you makes me want to be with you all the time. And I'm sorry if I'm making you uncomfortable, but I had to get that off my chest." Lily smiled and leaned in closer to meet James' gaze.

"I've never been a side piece before. I despise cheaters. And yet, here we are." James sat back up straight and took another sip of his drink. He instantly knew he had a problem on his hands. It sounded like Lily was going to be a willing participant in this affair. Without blunt clarification, James wouldn't be able to sleep tonight, so he had to ask.

"Does this mean what I think this means?" Lily sat upright, too.

"It means I'm down for a good time. I haven't had fun in a long time. I've been building my practice and putting off dating for the past ten years." She leaned in again to whisper. "And, believe it or not, that was the first orgasm that I didn't give myself in years." She leaned back towards her food again and picked up another fry. "I'm due for some fun." She raised her fry hand and pushed it towards James as a stop sign. "But only fun. I'm not looking to catch feelings, and I definitely don't want this to blow up in our faces." James was taken aback. It's exactly what he wanted to hear and exactly what he wanted. Dr. Michaels said he could pursue this feeling as long as he wasn't falling in love. And it sounded like Lily just agreed to the unspoken terms he'd created in his mind.

"Wow! That was really forward." Lily stopped eating and looked at James as if she'd said something wrong.

"Oh no. Did I misread the situation?" Lily's eyes got really big with worry.

"No. Not at all. My 'wow' was because I wasn't expecting you to be so forward, let alone open to what I wanted. Let me be clear, this is exactly what I want." Lily let out a sigh of relief. "Sorry, I didn't mean to make you doubt that."

"Listen. We can take things as fast or as slow as you want. Just as long as we stick to the agreement. No feelings." James put his hand out to shake her hand.

"Deal!" Lily extended her hand and shook James' hand firmly.

"Deal!" She then took a $50 bill out of her wallet and laid it on the counter. She waved to flag the waitress across the counter at the end. "Thank you." She tapped the bill for her to see and gave her another wave. Then she turned to James. "You're going to be late to our meeting, sir." She then took one last, long sip of her milkshake and put the cup down on the counter. She turned and walked directly out of the door leaving James there in awe. She never looked back.

The Start

The after school program was going well. It seemed like it was helping a lot of single mothers in the community, and petty crimes in the area decreased by 20%. James watched from the far end of the fellowship hall as Lily used her stethoscope on a little boy. She had a lovely smile on her face that showed the pure joy in what she was doing. It had been three months since the program started, and the once a week he got to see her was just enough to keep James wanting more. It has also been three months since they agreed to be secret lovers, but nothing physical had happened between them since that afternoon in the office. James stared in her direction hoping she would look up and make eye contact with him. She was so involved with her new patients and that's all she focused on. Saul walked up from the opposite direction of James' gaze and patted him on the back. "Hey Pastor. How's it going today?" James turned to look at Saul who was looking past him and at Lily.

"Hey Saul. It's going great! That Lily is someone special, huh?" James asked, knowing the answer.

"Yeah, she is. I wish she would give me a chance. We had one date, but she must not have been feeling me because she makes all kinds of excuses when I ask her to go out again." Saul shook his head in disappointment.

"Where have you asked her to go?" James inquired.

"I've tried Oak Steakhouse, Sullivan's, for the live music vibes, Kabutos, I even tried the Fig Tree. She turned me down every time." Saul hung his head in shame.

"Maybe you're trying too hard to impress her. Why don't you dial it down and ask her to go somewhere simple. I know she loves the Panthers. Ask her to go to a game. Or we're in full winter, why don't you take her to the mountains to see some snow. Alice and I love being cozy in our car while we drive up the snow-capped mountains and see the views. I can't keep Alice's hands off me after that move." Saul thought about it for a minute then hung his head again.

"Naw, Pastor. A man can't take but so much rejection in his lifetime. I'll find the right one. It'll just take a little more searchin'. But in the meantime, she is nice to look at, huh?" James wanted to agree in the worst way, but he couldn't let on how he couldn't stop thinking about, even lusting after, the beautiful Lily. James patted Saul on the shoulder with his heartfelt sympathy and walked away. Saul stood there admiring Lily a little longer before he turned and walked towards the church office.

After the line dwindled, it looked like Lily was seeing the last few children. James wandered in Lily's direction, still hoping to catch her eye. She finally looked up and saw him staring. She smiled a lovely smile and then turned her attention back to the last little girl standing in front of her. She gave the girl a big hug and she ran off to play with her friends. Lily stood from her seat and stretched. Her knees were sore from sitting all day, so she kicked out both legs and shook off the rust. She wore a long, mustard dress underneath her lab coat. Her flat, brown, knee-length boots ran up her long legs, but James realized that was the first time he'd seen her without heels. Even in flats, she was still noticeably tall. James admired her from afar trying not to be obvious. He high-fived several children as he walked in her direction. He peeked over their shoulders and complemented their artwork, playing the role of the proud pastor, but really, he needed to make his way to Lily. He needed to hear what she was going to say about why they hadn't seen each other over the past three months. Lily was standing by herself with her hands crossed behind her back. She was waiting and watching as James made his way across the room to her. "Good afternoon, Doc. How'd it go today?" James asked as he drew closer.

"Good afternoon, Pastor. It was a huge success, as usual." Lily smiled a confident smile. "I'm ready to discuss expanding the program whenever you are." Lily pointed around the fellowship hall. "We have plenty of space to grow, and I think adding another 50 students would be in order." James followed Lily's point and noticed there was plenty of space to expand.

"I think we could talk about that. Would you like to come to my office to discuss this or should we find a more appropriate place this time?" James threw her a sly, sexy smile to go along with his obvious proposition. Lily smiled right back at him. She reached into her lab coat and pulled out a small, square object. She handed it to James and walked away. James looked at his hand. It was a Quality Inn hotel key card in a sleeve. The room number, 108, was written on the front of the sleeve. The hotel address was printed on the back of the card. It was a Kings Mountain address, which was about a 35 minute drive from Charlotte. James pulled his phone out from his back pocket and searched the internet for the address. It was a motel-style place that was right off of I-85 South. The room she chose was strategic. It was towards the back of the hotel, away from the street and the lobby. James could park right outside the room and run in without anyone seeing him or his car there. James was surprised by the amount of thought she put into this adventure. Here he was thinking she was avoiding him, but she'd carefully plotted their first real rendezvous. James turned to see where Lily had gone. She was across the room and escorting the children towards the exit. James looked at his watch. It was time for the children to go home. Was Lily expecting him to meet her there now or later in the evening? He was confused and excited at the same time. It was so spontaneous to him, but something Lily had planned. It was the first time in his life that someone had caught him off guard this way.

James received a *ding* on his smart watch. It was a text message from Alice telling him that she and the boys were going to dinner and the play at the high school with a group of friends. She texted that dinner was on the stove for when he got home. James wiped his eyes in disbelief. How was this all falling into place right now? Did Lily know this was play night? Again, the confusion set in on his face. James was frozen in the moment. He didn't know if he was ready for all of this to happen so fast. Five minutes ago, James would have relished the moment, but now that it was real, James was thinking he would coward out. All of the children and adults were in the lobby of the fellowship hall waiting for parent pick-up to be over. There were only a handful of kids left, but the adults outnumbered the kids. James looked out of the glass doors to see Lily standing in the parking lot talking to a boy and his mother. He sent salutations to the people in the lobby and walked out the door. Lily heard the door open and quickly ended her conversation. She walked towards James. James continued in her direction while looking around to make sure no ears could hear.

"Ready?" Lily asked as she reached within arms-length of James.

"Now?" James asked.

"Yeah now. Unless you're having second thoughts." Lily said with a smile.

"No, I'm good." James said with hesitation.

"I'm sorry. Is this too much too soon? I just heard my patients talking about how much of a big deal the play at the school was going to be on Friday night, and I figured that would eliminate anyone looking for us." James took a deep breath and smiled.

"It's kind of nice to hear you were thinking about me. I do so much for everyone else. I'm the planner. So it's nice to see the roles reversed."

"Listen, why don't we go get something to eat. There's a Waffle House right in front of the hotel. Why don't we eat and talk, and whatever happens after that happens. I'm cool either way."

"How *are* you so cool?" James asked with a smile.

"I'm a doctor, remember? I'm always cool." Lily turned towards her car and began to walk away. James called after her.

"And don't think for a minute I'm going to let this whole Waffle House thing slide. You're a rich and prestigious doctor and all I get is some Waffle House?"

"I told you I'm a simple girl. That's one of my favorite places to eat. Give me a pecan waffle and some scattered, covered, and smothered hash browns, and I'm in heaven." They both laughed as they made their way to their cars. James got into his car and reached for his phone. He realized he didn't text Alice back. He sent her a quick "ok" and started the car. Lily pulled out of her space first and made a right out of the church complex. James waited a minute. It was his moment of truth, and he wanted to make sure his mind, and his heart were all in on this decision. This was his moment at the crossroads. He could either put the car in drive and turn right to follow Lily or he could turn left and go home to the meal his wife made him. James didn't take this decision lightly. His impulse to pleasure Lily on his desk a few months back wasn't planned. He could chalk it up to being in the spur of the moment, but this was a different moment. He was making a conscious decision to start an affair. However, many times it would happen was unknown to him at this time, but he knew this was the moment of truth.

James started the ignition but left the car in park. Lily's car was out of sight at this point, so he had a minute to think. James couldn't help but to feel guilty. As would any man in his situation. It wasn't like he and Alice were unhappy. He had no excuses. This decision was purely selfish. James thought about how he'd never been a selfish man in the past, yet he was about to do something so unexpected, so bold, so selfish, and so out of character. He didn't want to be a cliche. He didn't want to fit into the "every man cheats" category as so many women had placed men in the past. James put his hand on the gear shift and put the car in drive. He crept forward to the street and put his blinker on. James made a left turn towards home. That was where he needed to go, and that's what he decided to do.

As he rolled into the street, he heard the sound of a horn honking emphatically. James looked to the left where the sound was coming from and realized he had pulled out in front of a semi-truck that was still barreling down the road, unable to stop. James swerved his car hard to the right and accelerated as hard as he could. The truck barely missed him, as James grabbed his heart and blew out a sigh of relief. The truck honked again from behind him, reminding him of how poorly he had pulled into the road. In all his distraction, he hadn't realized he was traveling towards the interstate and not towards home. Was it a sign? Was he supposed to be heading towards Lily and not towards Alice? James turned right onto the on-ramp and merged onto I-85 South. The decision had been made for him. He was going to meet Lily for a breakfast dinner. He knew what was going to come next, but he agreed to himself that he'd take one step at a time.

Lily was sitting in a booth when James pulled up. He had to admit to himself, he was nervous. He knew he exuded confidence outwardly, but on the inside, he was a screaming mess. James walked into the Waffle House and sat in the booth. The waitress came just in the nick of time before he had a chance to say how much of a mistake it was for him to be there. "Can I get ya some water, honey?" She asked in her very southern accent.

"Yes, please." Lily replied sweetly. The waitress placed a menu down in front of her and James, and then walked away quickly to grab the water. James needed some water to clear the lump in his throat. He questioned himself the entire way down the road. *Why was she doing this? Of all the men in all of Charlotte, why was she choosing me?* Even at the sight of them together, people would label her a homewrecker. She'd forever be a mistress. She didn't plan to be the object of James' attention, but somehow, she was. And it didn't make sense to him. He had the most beautiful wife. His sons were chiseled out of stone as perfect specimens in the making, and yet here he was sitting inside a Waffle House to meet her.

The waitress came back with the water and a straw. James quickly unwrapped the straw and gulped down several ounces of water. "Nope, still there." He said aloud.

"What was that, darlin'?" The waitress asked, bending over to hear James better.

"Nothing." James took another long sip of his water and finally made eye contact with Lily. James loved the way that Lily looked. She was so incredibly beautiful, and her voice reminded him of Eartha Kitt as Cat Woman. It was soulful and rich, and every word sounded like she was saying something sexy, even when she wasn't.

Lily felt drawn to him, too. It wasn't like she'd planned to seduce him. She had every intention of starting an afterschool program with him and making her community better. Her intentions were very professional, yet she received the biggest birthday surprise of them all; a tryst with a gorgeous man. From that moment on, she tried to avoid James. Even though she wanted to keep their agreement at the diner, she couldn't stop thinking about that day in his office. How strong his hands were as they felt their way around her body. How soft his lips were when he kissed hers. Even with the force of him pressing up against her, he was still surprisingly gentle. Their sexual chemistry was undeniable, but the way he knew his way around her body was surprising. It's as if he'd studied her physique in a classroom before he'd even touched her. Her body was on fire from that moment until now. Every time she saw him in the fellowship hall, she'd have to avoid his gaze because all it took was one look or one smile to make her feel like her skin needed his touch.

"You ready to order?" James asked shyly.

"I have a rotation of what I get from here, but you can take your time to order. I'm good." James studied the menu for a while. Lily watched from the top of his head as he looked down at the menu. He could hear the faint sounds of sizzling from the grill in the background and chatter all around the restaurant, but it was all white noise to him. The loudest audible sound to him was his own breathing. He felt like his heart was beating a mile a minute. This was a feeling he wasn't used to - panic. James was always sure of himself. Confident, even. But Lily made him feel out of control. Like she'd cast a spell on him. It was like when the old voodoo mamas would bury their husbands' underwear in the yard so they couldn't leave home. They were just as stuck as he was. The waitress walked over and stood by the table without saying a word. James looked up and smiled at her and then looked back down at the menu. "We're going to need a minute." Lily told the waitress.

"Sure." She responded and walked away.

"Are you nervous?" Lily asked as she looked at James. "I'm feeling nervous for the first time in a long while. I'm not used to this feeling, if I'm being totally honest." James finally looked up to make eye contact with Lily.

"Yes. If I'm being honest, I wasn't going to come. I was headed home and almost got into an accident. It's like the car was telling me to come to you." Lily's face turned into one of worry.

"Oh my goodness! Are you ok?"

"I'm fine. The turbo engine seemed like it had jets. I put my foot through the floor and it took off." They both laughed. "Listen, I honestly don't know why I'm here. I love my wife, and I'm never leaving her. So, I don't know where this is going or if there's even a point to get started." Lily smiled in relief.

"I would be concerned if you didn't have second thoughts. That just means you're a good guy with a conscience. That's why I said, we can just eat and chill. If we feel like we want to move forward, then we have a room right behind the restaurant.

If not, 85 is right there, and we can go home." James thought for a minute.

"No strings attached?" James asked as a final question.

"No strings." Lily responded.

"Then let's get out of here." James stood up and put his hand out to help Lily from the booth. She took his hand to help herself up. He took a $20 bill out of his wallet and put it on the table for the waitress. Lily saw the gesture and felt her face flush. That was the sexiest thing she'd seen in a long time. She knew he had a generous heart. It was obvious that he was a good human being, which made him a good pastor and member of the community. It was everything about James that turned her on. He was the kind of man she would have loved to have meet her parents, God rest their souls, and forage a life with. But Lily's life was far too complicated to settle down right now. She had always put her ambitions before her love life. So, while her friends and family were getting married and starting families, she was knee deep in establishing her practice. Yes, it got lonely after a while, but her desire for professional success and status in the community far outweighed her desire for a man. Of course, she had needs, but that's what the Rabbit 2.0 was for. It was fast, efficient, and convenient. She didn't have to put lingerie on for it or spend time getting to know it. She didn't have to play Russian Roulette if the rabbit was going to have the stamina, size, and girth she desired to please her. She could put on her favorite tube channel for foreplay and pleasure herself on demand. 100% satisfaction guaranteed or her money back. And yet, she was hand-in-hand with the man of her fantasies feeling her entire body yearn for him in the middle of a Waffle House.

"Ma'am. We're going to head out. Sorry for the inconvenience." James said as he and Lily walked towards the door. James slowed his pace to let Lily pass him. He reached out and pushed the door open for Lily to walk through first. Lily turned to face James as she used her backside to push the second door open. James walked up to her and grabbed her by the waist, pulling her close to his face. He kissed her lips softly with the sweetest peck. James licked the kiss from his lips. She tasted like cherry chapstick. Just another thing he was fond of. Something as subtle as chapstick flavor told James that Lily really was someone special. James grabbed Lily's hand and walked her over to her car. He opened the door for her and placed her in the driver's seat.

"Following you." He said as he closed the door. Lily started the engine. All of the nerves he felt seemed to have left his body. He was starting to get excited about the prospect of having someone else work to please him. Lily looked out her passenger side window to see if James had made it to his car. He was closing the door, so she put the car in reverse and backed out of the space and towards the back of the restaurant where the hotel was just over a hundred yards away. She pulled her vehicle in front of room 108, leaving the space to the right of hers available for James to park. This would not only hide his car from the street, but it gave him more cover as he got out of his car and walked into the room. Lily opened her car door first and retrieved the hotel room key from her purse. She tucked her purse underneath the seat and grabbed her car keys. She didn't want to take the chance of leaving anything behind. She got out, closed her car door, and locked the car behind her as she walked towards the room. She opened the door with the key card and held it open for James. He quickly opened his door, hopped out, and trotted into the room. He locked his car from inside the hotel room.

James looked around the room. It wasn't the four or five star hotel he was used to, but it would do. It was a little more spacious than a normal hotel room. There was a sofa and an end table underneath the window next to the door. The king bed sat in the center of the room just a few feet away. There was an armoire with drawers that contained the television directly across from the bed and a work desk immediately to the right. James walked past the bed to look at the bathroom. The sink and mirror were on the outside of the tub and toilet room. James hated this set up. He always thought it was dumb to wake a sleeping person with the sound of the sink if he had to go to the bathroom in the middle of the night. His father was a loud snorer. When they went on vacation when he was a child, he would have to go to sleep first so as to not be disturbed by his snoring. It was inevitable that someone would wake him with the sound of handwashing in the middle of the night. Then, he couldn't go back to sleep because of the loud snores leaving his father's face. James peeked into the bathroom that was shoddily upgraded. He could see their effort, but all the seams and caulking were all wrong. It was a hotel room, for sure. The interior was clean, and that's all that mattered in the moment.

Lily had put a bottle of champagne in an ice bucket on the end table next to the sofa when she booked the room and retrieved the keys. The ice was now mostly melted but the bottle remained chilled. James noticed the bottle first.

"Did you plan on liquoring me up and taking advantage of me?" James asked jokingly.

"No, I was going to let you liquor me up. I'm a fun drunk." They both laughed. "Want me to open the bottle?" Lily asked, reaching for the bottle.

"No, allow me." James said as he reached for the bottle as well. Lily retracted her hand from the champagne bottle and reached for the two hotel room glasses to place them next to the ice bin. James peeled back the wrapper from the bottle and untied the cork foil. He struggled a little to pull the cork straight out of the bottle. Lily went to the sink to retrieve a hand towel. She placed the towel over the top of the cork and bottle for James.

"I find it less daunting when it's covered by a towel. You can twist and wiggle the cork out without the fear of losing an eye." James was grateful for the advice and used her technique. The cork came out with a *pop* and James poured the champagne into the waiting glasses. He lifted both glasses and handed one to Lily.

"Here's to a mutually satisfying experience." James held up his glass.

"Here's to mind-blowing sex and a memory that holds us until the next time." Lily clinked James' glass and they both took a sip. Lily put her glass back on the end table and sat on the sofa. "Now, strip." Lily demanded.

"Excuse me?" James asked, puzzled. "You want me to strip?" Lily laughed.

"Yes. We're not going to be cliche here. I want you to take your clothes off so I can see your naked form." James flashed Lily a sexy, confident smile. James knew he was a sight to admire, and he was happy to give Lily exactly what she wanted.

"Well all right." James said as he put down his glass next to Lily's. He pulled his shirt off slowly to reveal his rock hard abs and chiseled pecs. Lily looked at his chest and bit her lip with delight. James stepped out of his tennis shoes and placed them at the side of the bed, dropping the t-shirt on top of them. He then unbuttoned his pants to reveal his gray and black boxer brief underwear. He pulled them down slowly to reveal his bulge that was increasingly getting bigger. Lily felt her body getting warm. She knew she was in for a treat, but she didn't know exactly what to expect. James stepped out of his pants and dropped them on his clothes pile. "You sure you're ready for this?" James asked with a cocky attitude.

"I think I'll take my chances." Lily responded sarcastically. James pulled down his underwear and stepped out of them. He also added them to complete the pile of his clothes next to the bed. Lily admired James' naked body. She looked at his erect penis with delight. It was perfect! Like they should make a mold out of it and sell it in sex shops across the world. She saw the slight bend in it that made her curious if it could penetrate her walls and reach the spot on the top that made her feel like her eyes would forever roll in the back of her head and never return.

"Your turn." James demanded. Before she stood up, Lily unzipped her boots and stepped out. She grabbed her mustard dress and lifted it from the bottom. She pulled it up past her waist, revealing her purple panties. She kept pulling it over her equally impressive abs to show her lacy purple bra. Lily could hear James' breath begin to quicken as she pulled the dress over her head. It made her feel tingly to know that James liked what he saw. She let the dress fall to the floor and walked over to James. She wrapped her arms around his neck and whispered in his ear.

"I'm definitely liking what I see. But how does it feel?" James grabbed Lily's hand from around his neck and placed it on this throbbing member.

"You tell me." James said as he helped her stroke it. Lily gratefully obliged. Lily pushed James backwards until the back of his knees hit the bed. She gently pushed harder until he sat down on the bed. She climbed on top of him, as she grabbed the back of his head and pulled his face towards her.

"You're gonna be trouble, aren't you?" Lily asked sexily.

"Yes." James whispered as he kissed Lily passionately.

Andrea Furlow
The Planning

James woke up frantically. He had fallen asleep unintentionally. He rolled over towards the side of the bed and grabbed for the phone in his pants pocket. It was only 8:27 p.m., but James felt like he'd been asleep for hours. He rolled over to look at Lily but she wasn't there. He got up and walked over to the window. He peeked out and didn't see Lily's car. He looked around the room for a note or any signs of Lily but there was nothing. James went to the sink and splashed some water on his face. He looked at himself in the mirror. James looked down at his happily dangling friend and smiled. He had just finished taking the most intimate advantage of Lily's body, and he'd done some of his finest work if he'd say so himself. Just then he heard the door slam. James turned around, startled by the sound. "Am I interrupting something?" Lily called from the door. She was standing there with Waffle House bags in her hand. James hung his head and laughed into his chest as he walked over to her. He kissed her on the lips and grabbed a bag.

"What do we have here?" James asked as he looked into the bag in his hand. He started pulling out the to-go boxes.

"I didn't know if you wanted breakfast or dinner stuff, so I got a combination of both." Lily pulled the food out of her bag too. "I got a chicken salad." Lily handed James the chicken salad bowl with a packet of salad dressing on the top. "I got a plain waffle and a pecan waffle. I didn't know if you had food allergies, so I didn't want to assume you could eat the pecan." James smiled.

"No, no food allergies here." James assured her.

"Ok good. I also got bacon, turkey bacon, and sausage patties." Lily tapped the lid of each container as she explained what was in it.

"Turkey bacon for me please." James requested. Lily made a face of disgust in his direction. "What?" James asked with a laugh. "I actually prefer the taste of turkey bacon. I'm a pork sausage guy, but I just don't like pork bacon." Lily turned up her nose again.

"This was fun while it lasted." Lily joked. James moved the food out of the way and launched himself at Lily.

"Oh really. I'm being dumped over my bacon choices?" James wrapped his arms around Lily and put his entire weight on top of her. Lily tried to resist the much larger man, but she finally went limp.

"No! Now get off me so I can eat. I'm starving." James got up and laughed.

"I'm going to eat real quick and head off, if you don't mind. I want to get home before Alice and the kids get back."

"Sure." Lily replied. She opened the pecan waffle and started to cut into it in large pieces. She stuffed one large piece into her mouth and chewed it ferociously.

"Dang, you are hungry." James joked. Lily picked up a salt packet and threw it at him.

"After that fast and furious session, yeah, I'm famished." Lily winked at James as he blushed. James responded in the most southern accent he could find.

"Aw shucks, ma'am. Much obliged." Lily found the pepper packet and threw that at him too. James caught it. "Thanks." He said with a laugh. Lily took another large bite of waffle. James heard a buzz from his phone. He walked over to the bed where he'd left it to see a text message from Alice. She said the play was over, but the boys wanted to go get ice cream. He looked up at Lily who was staring back at him anticipating the news. "Do you mind if I jump in the shower and take my food to go?" Lily smiled a sympathetic smile. She didn't respond with anything other than a nod, tipping her imaginary cowboy hat. She then took another bite of her waffle.

James walked into the bathroom and turned on the water. He waited for it to get hot and then stepped in. He rinsed his body off with only the water and his hands. He turned off the water and stepped out of the shower grabbing a towel on the way out of the bathroom. He was still dripping wet, and he walked back towards Lily. "What, no soap? And did you forget how to dry off? You think you're back in the locker room again?" Lily said with a laugh.

"No soap. You can't walk in the door after being gone all day and smell like a fresh bar of soap. And I like to air dry." James tossed the towel in Lily's direction. Lily deflected the towel onto the ground.

"I packed the salad and a waffle for you. Don't forget to dispose of it in the garbage bin and not your kitchen trash." James put his clothes on and tucked his phone in his pocket. He looked around the room to make sure he hadn't forgotten anything. "Your keys are over there on the desk." Lily pointed to the corner of the work desk where James' keys were resting. He walked over and grabbed his keys. He then scanned the room one last time as he walked over to Lily. She stood up, handed him the bag of food and tilted her forehead for James to kiss it. James obliged and kissed Lily's head with a quick peck. "Thanks for the good time. This was fun." Lily said excitedly.

"Was it as mind-blowing and memorable as you wanted?" James asked.

"More than." Lily replied with a breathy whisper. James kissed her forehead again and walked towards the door. Lily sat back down to finish her food.

James unlocked his car and walked hastily towards the driver's side door. He looked around but the hotel lot was deserted. It was the perfect place. The hotel wasn't too busy, and it was blocked from street view by the Waffle House in front. He got into the car and quickly backed out to head home. He put on the GPS, and it said there were 37 minutes until he'd arrive at home. That was plenty of time to beat Alice and the kids. James opened the salad and began to pick up and eat the pieces of dry lettuce and chicken.

James merged onto the highway, and for the first time he'd thought about what just transpired. He had just tangled with another woman for the first time since he and Alice first started dating. He'd never even considered it before Lily and now he couldn't think of life without that experience. Lily wasn't widely experienced, James could tell by her movements in bed, but she let him lead her in a way that made him feel like he was in control. With every push, she pushed back, with every stroke, she'd stroke back, and with every touch, she'd touch back. They were in sync. That's something he'd never experienced with Alice. Of course, Alice was a wild and amazing lover. He wouldn't have married her if she wasn't. But Alice was a woman who knew her body. She was there to please herself which in turn pleased James. Lily was different. She took her pleasure from pleasing James. That was a turn on to him which made him want to please her even more. Plus, the sense of naughtiness around the whole situation heightened the sense of electricity Lily brought into the bedroom.

James cruised down the highway feeling like a new man. He had visions of Lily's soft lips kissing his ears and his neck. He could feel his hands around her back, hugging her body tightly as she rode him up and down. Her long legs wrapped around his waist as he turned her onto her back. It was all a vision that he wanted again, but he knew it wasn't something that could happen for a long while. He didn't want to lie to Alice or make excuses for where he was going if he wanted to see Lily again. He wanted their time together to be, relatively, guilt-free.

James pulled into the garage. He'd beaten his family home. He dumped the Waffle House bag into the garbage bin in the garage and rushed into the house. He made a beeline to the kitchen to wrap up and put away the food Alice had left for him on the stove. It looked like stir-fried chicken and vegetables, which was one of his favorites, but that's not what James would have chosen for himself on a Friday night. He then went upstairs to take a proper shower. He wished he could leave Lily's scent on him, but that would have been bad news for his marriage. James grabbed some pajama pants and a t-shirt from his drawer and headed towards the bathroom. He could hear the sound of his sons coming into the house, as he closed the bathroom door. He hung his bed clothes on the hook where his towel usually goes and walked into the shower. He turned on the rain shower and didn't wait for the water to warm up. He stuck his head under the cool water and let it run through his hair. "Hey babe, we're back." Alice called from the door.

"Hey, how'd it go?" James asked through the water.

"It was good for a high school play. The fellas and their friends liked it a lot. Sorry you couldn't come. How was the program today?" Alice inquired.

"It was good. Dr. Lily asked if we could increase the attendance by another 50 kids." Alice walked all the way in the door and closed it behind her. "What do you think?" James asked, still through the water as he reached for his soap.

"I think it's a great idea. Do you have the capacity and volunteers to accommodate another 50?" Alice asked, knowing the answer.

"I think so."

"Then I think you have your answer." Alice replied, logically. "We've had doctors. Do you think we should add a dentist to the rotation? You know Ears' new coach Eric is a dentist by day. You haven't met him yet, but he seems like a pretty good dude. He may be interested in volunteering once or twice a month. Especially in the off season."

"That's a good idea. I think I have his number, but can you text it to me just in case?" James' words cut off as he washed his face.

"Sure. And I'll put a bug in his ear at practice on Monday."

"Sounds good, honey. Thank you." James said with gratitude.

"You're very welcome. I'm going to make sure the boys get settled ok and head to bed. See you soon?" Alice asked in a sexy voice.

"Yes ma'am. I'll see you soon." James forgot about the idea of having to please two women. He was pretty tired after the first romp in the sheets, but now he had to match Alice's energy. She wasn't a woman who went for the fast version. James finished washing his body and took a long rinse. He wasn't stalling for time, but he wasn't exactly rushing out of the bathroom. He took his time. He turned the water off and went to get a towel from the linen closet. He patted himself dry because he didn't want to wet the sheets. He dropped the towel in the laundry basket and grabbed his pajamas on the way out of the bathroom.

Alice was already in bed when James arrived. She looked at him with her bedroom eyes. James smiled lovingly at his beautiful wife. Her face was angelic at the moment. It wasn't often that he stopped to admire her beauty. Yes, she was beautiful, but James didn't tell her often enough. "You look like an angel, my love." James said with admiration. Alice smiled a coy smile and then let out the biggest yawn. James looked at her with confusion.

"I'm so sorry, babe. That was totally unexpected."

"If you're tired, we can make love in the morning. I know how you love some good Saturday morning lovin'.." James joked.

"That sounds nice. I didn't get tired until I laid down. Are you mad?" Alice asked with sad eyes.

"Of course not, it's been a long week for both of us. Come here." James climbed over Alice to his side of the bed, making her giggle. He grabbed her and spooned her tightly. "You comfortable?" James asked as he nestled his face into her back and made himself comfortable.

"Yes. I love you, James." Alice said softly.

"I love you too." James said as he drifted off to sleep. He knew he'd dodged double duty, but he was grateful to come home to Alice, even after being with Lily. He knew where his home was - with Alice and the kids - but he also knew that Lily was a part of him now. Being with her completed his happiness with such an unexpected, dangerous pleasure he didn't know he wanted or needed. But what he did know is, at that moment, he was going to sleep peacefully.

James woke up as the sunlight peeked over the horizon. He kissed Alice's back and grabbed his cell phone as he went into the bathroom. He relieved himself and washed his hands. As he was drying his hands off, he saw he had a text message from Lester, his pastor mentor from Jackson, Mississippi. It read:

Hey J. Having a conference next month. Wanna speak for a hefty honorarium?

James thought about it for a moment. That meant he would spend the weekend in Jackson. It would be the perfect time for James to spend a few days with Lily. He replied to his mentor with a yes and asked if he could bring a friend. Unexpectedly, James' phone rang immediately after he sent the message. It was Lester. James pressed the button on the side of the phone to make it go silent. He crept back through the bedroom past the still sleeping Alice and out the bedroom door. He tiptoed down the stairs and finally pressed the green answer button. "Hello?" James asked in a whisper.

"Hey man. It's Les. What guest you talkin' bout? You didn't say can I bring my wife or my kids or my friend. You said a guest. Who we talkin' bout?"

"Well hello to you too. I'm fine. Thanks for asking." James said defiantly. "And for the record, it's a..." James looked around to make sure no one else was awake or around before he continued. "Female friend." He finished in a whisper.

"A female friend you're having relations with or just a friend." Lester inquired with a jest in his voice.

"A friend with benefits." James answered hesitantly. He waited for Lester to judge him. He wanted Lester to judge him. Here Lester was asking him to preach in his first out-of-town conference for a "hefty honorarium" and all he could think about was getting laid again by Lily.

"I see." Lester said, but there wasn't any judgment in his voice. "Well, if it's going to be that kind of party, then I'm going to make a few more arrangements." James was confused. Was Lester condoning his behavior?

"What kind of arrangements?" James inquired.

"Just arrangements." James was intrigued. He'd always thought of Lester to be a straight and narrow guy. Yet, it sounded like he was about to organize some bad behavior.

"Nothing crazy, right?" James asked as he felt his heart beating with nerves.

"Naw man, nothing you wouldn't want to do. Trust me. We all have limits, and I would never push yours. Just trust me." James agreed and hung up the phone. He looked at the time and relished in the fact that the house was quiet. It felt peaceful. He walked into the kitchen and opened the fridge. He poked around for a little bit, but he didn't find anything that appetized him. It was almost time for the house to start buzzing, so he made himself some coffee in his single-cup-brewer. James wasn't really a coffee guy, but he did enjoy it every once in a while. He took a sip, but it was too hot. He set the cup down on the counter and picked up his cell phone. He dialed Lily's number. "Good morning." She answered with a smile so obvious James could hear it through the phone.

"Good morning." James was happy to hear that his phone call was greeted with such delight. "I wanted to thank you for the good time and food last night. And, I was hoping to entice you into doing it again."

"What did you have in mind?" Lily asked, still vocally smiling.

"I'm heading to Jackson next month for a conference. Care to join me for the weekend?" The phone went silent. James didn't hear the click that the call had ended but he also didn't hear Lily anymore. He started to worry. "Hello?" Lily spoke up to break the silence that was concerning James.

"I'm sorry. You couldn't hear my happy dance. Yes. I'd love to come. You can tell me the details this week when I see you after program."

"That sounds like a plan." James said, with a sigh of relief. "Oh, by the way, Alice wants to bring in a dentist to donate his time once or twice a month. What do you think?" Lily answered right away.

"I think it's great. Dental health is just as important as physical health. They go hand in hand." Lily sounded excited by the prospect of expanding services to the children.

"Then it's a deal. We'll talk this week."

"Ok." Lily said as James hung up the phone. He put his phone down on the counter and picked up his cup of coffee. He took a sip and headed towards the stairs. He enjoyed the prospect of making Lily happy. She had filled the last few months with good vibes, but last night was the culmination of something that was a long time in the making. James walked back up the stairs with a smile on his face. He opened the door and looked over at Alice. She was text messaging on her phone. She looked up and smiled at James.

"What are you so cheerful about this morning?" Alice asked.

"Just looking at my beautiful wife." Alice blushed. James walked over, set his coffee cup on the nightstand, and climbed into bed. He slithered sexily over to Alice and kissed her arm. He kissed her in line to her neck, and Alice giggled like a schoolgirl.

"Sorry baby. We're going to have to take another raincheck. I have to meet the deaconess at the church. Something about approving the budget for the Christmas program and the children's costumes." James rolled over onto his pillow and let out a loud sigh of annoyance. Alice laughed and laid her head on his chest. "I know, baby." Alice lamented, as she kissed his cheek. "But we don't have any plans tonight. Let's send the boys to their friends' houses and snuggle up on the couch and watch a scary movie. I'll make some movie theater popcorn and add a sprinkle of parmesan like you like it." Alice rubbed her nose against James' cheek. James responded with a smile and a kiss on the lips.

"Sure." James played like he was mad, but he was perfectly fine with the plan. He loved making Alice feel guilty for something she had no control over. That just made the sex even better when she promised. She would give him her best moves to *make up for* whatever it was that seemingly offended him.

Alice got up and went to the bathroom to get dressed. James stayed in bed. He thought about the offer to preach for the conference in Jackson. It was his chance to create a sermon that would put him in front of some very noted, national pastors' radars. He didn't want to mess up the opportunity to shine for future conferences. They usually paid the pastors an honorarium and then take up an offering if the pastor did a good job. That could be anywhere from a couple hundred dollars to a couple thousand dollars depending on the attendance and his sermon. It could also legitimize him as a pastor. There were days he felt like an imposter, but James knew he was good at making people feel motivated to do good things for themselves and for the community. He taught about creating wealth and a wealthy mindset, which seemed to fare well with his patrons. So, that was an obvious theme, but how would he spin it for the Jackson crowd. James put his hands behind his head and rested them on top of his pillow. Alice came out of the bathroom and saw her husband in deep thought. "A penny for your thoughts." James looked over at her and smiled lovingly. James knew Alice always had a good solution, so he decided to ask her thoughts.

"Lester called me this morning. He asked me to speak at his conference in Jackson next month." Alice squealed with excitement, ran over to James, and jumped in the bed. She landed with a flop.

"That's great news! Do you want me to come for moral support?" James rolled to his side to face Alice.

"No, that's ok. I appreciate the offer. I would like your help with the sermon part, though. What would you choose as a subject?" Alice thought out loud for a minute.

"Let's see. Jackson in January. Church conference. Lester is a great orator, so you'll have to be pretty clever with your words, but not overly wordy. Hmm. New Year, New You? New Year, New Money? New Year, New Things? Never. Hmm." Alice laid her head on James' chest while she continued to speak her thoughts aloud. "New Dawn, New Day? It has to be something that relates to the new year. People make their resolutions, but by the end of January, they've broken them." James thought about what Alice was saying, and it was true. People always have high expectations for the new year but rarely have a plan.

"What about 'New Approach'? Like, stop doing the same old thing and expecting something new. Try a new approach." Alice thought about it for a second. James could see she wasn't sold on the idea, so he elaborated further. "Why don't I give them a five-step-plan on how to plan and achieve their resolutions by taking a new approach." Alice pointed her index finger to the ceiling.

"By golly, I think you've got it." She said in a Scottish accent. James put his fingers under Alice's armpits and tickled her. Alice quickly squirmed out of position so James couldn't reach her and threw him a love punch on his shoulder. "I think that's it, my love. I'm headed out but keep me posted on how things go. You know I'm happy to help." James smiled a half smile and gave Alice a nod. She climbed out of bed, adjusted her clothes, and headed towards the bedroom door. "Love you, babe." She said as she hurried through the door, looking at her watch. "Be home later." James watched as she walked out of the door.

The Beginning of the End

James stepped off of the plane to a cold chill. There was a gust of wind that crept through the small opening between the plane and the jetway that filled the tunnel like a cold slap in the face. James hurried along the corridor into the main terminal with a trot, rolling his carry-on bag behind him. He instructed Lily to take a separate airline that arrived at the same time as his flight to avoid them crossing paths at the Charlotte airport. It wasn't a genius plan, but it also ensured that no one would see them together. She'd been waiting for about 30 minutes, according to the text message she sent him when she landed. He didn't know why his flight took longer than expected, but he also wasn't paying attention. He'd replayed his sermon over again in his mind. He'd rehearsed all week and was prepared, but his nerves were starting to get the best of him.

Lester's driver was picking him up, but he wanted to meet Lily at baggage claim first. James reached the terminal doorway and immediately spotted a sign with an arrow pointing him in the direction of baggage claim. He followed the sign to the escalator. There were lots of travelers around which made for a nice traffic jam at the escalator entry point. He anticipated his turn behind an elderly couple traveling with a screaming toddler. The child didn't want to get on the escalator and fell down on the floor blocking the flow of traffic. Embarrassed, the couple tried to pick up the child who'd gone limp on the floor still whaling in agony as if someone had pinched him. Onlookers stood by annoyed as there was no passing this tragic display of grandparenting. James heard the sweetest voice behind him. "Excuse me." He could recognize that voice from anywhere. He turned to see Lily's lovely, smiling face. She made her way through the crowd to the front of the escalator where the child was still pitching a fit. She crouched down to the floor and whispered something to the child. Without any further protest, the child got up, grabbed the elderly man's hand, and the throuple headed down the escalator with no further incident. The sounds of clapping from behind them was thunderous.

Lily reached back for her roller, carry-on bag and boarded the escalator with the masses. She stepped off and to the right at the end before she looked back for James. James watched Lily the whole way down the escalator. She never ceased to amaze him. He wondered, the whole way down the escalator, what she had said to the kid to get him to get up. "What in the world just happened?" James asked with a look of astonishment on his face. Lily smiled and turned her face in an effort to play shy.

"I deal with kids' tantrums all day. I'm immune to crying. You know what works every time?" Lily quizzed. "Bribery."

"Bribery?" James asked. "Like, you bribed the kid to get him to stop crying?" James laughed as he asked the question because, as a father of four, he knew bribery didn't work until a certain age.

"Absolutely! You missed the part where I slipped him a lollipop and told him he could have his treat when he got home if he got up right now."

"Oh, so now you're the granny at church giving out unwrapped candy from your purse?" James teased. Lily pushed James' arm playfully. James rubbed his arm as if she'd done him harm. "And now you're the granny handing out spankings to other people's misbehaving children." Lily balled up her fist as if she was really going to hit him. "Ok, ok woman. I give. I give. What can I say? You're incredible." James put his hand on the small of her back to escort her toward the terminal exit. Lester said his driver would be waiting on them at baggage claim at 4:00 p.m. James looked at his watch which read 4:07 p.m. "The driver should be here. Let's see where the town car drivers are gathered to see if someone is looking for us." Lily pointed in the direction that appeared to be people waiting with signs. Just then James felt a tap on his shoulder.

"Anybody need a ride?" James looked back to see a short, stubby, and gray-haired man looking up at him.

"Lester!" James shouted as he gave him a hug. Lester wasn't a memorable man. He looked to be in his late 50's or early 60's.

Although he wasn't attractive, he wasn't unattractive either. He looked like any other man walking down the street, as his clothes and shoes were clearly off of a rack at a department store. No one would guess it by his appearance, but Lester was one of the wealthiest and influential men in Jackson, Mississippi. He was the senior pastor at the largest megachurch in the state and recently widowed. In all their excitement to see each other, James and Lester didn't pay attention to the two beautiful women standing behind them.

"Uh hum." Lily cleared her throat loudly as if to ask for a proper introduction. The woman behind Lester pushed past the two men to introduce herself. In her very southern accent, she said.

"You'll have to excuse ole Lester here. He's forgotten all of his manners in this moment of excitement. My name is Jillian Gray. I'm Lester's flavor of the week." Lester stopped laughing and hugging James and looked at Jillian with a frown.

"Why, that's not true at all." Lester replied in his own deeply southern accent. He walked over to Jillian and gave her a loving hug. He looked up at James and nodded as if to say it was true, but he didn't want Jillian to know it. "You mean a lot more to me than that. You're just fishin' for compliments." Lester rubbed his nose against Jillian's cheek as she blushed and kissed his cheek in return. Lily looked at James as she tried to conceal her smile. James interrupted their moment.

"This is Lily, and I'm James, and we're starving! You guys up for something to eat?" James asked, rubbing his stomach.

"Ooooo daddy! We should take them to Johnny T's for an early dinner. They have the blues band playin' all night tonight. Y'all like soul food?" Jillian didn't give anyone a chance to answer as she started pulling Lester towards the exit. Jillian was clearly younger than Lester. She was in her early 30's and had way too much spunk for an older, unremarkable person like Lester. Her hair was black, but she had a gray patch purposely colored in the front. Her calf-high combat boots clunked on the floor as she walked. Her half goth, half rocker look was unique yet well put together. Again, obviously too young and hip for Lester, but somehow this unlikely couple seemed to get along well.

The group walked out of the terminal doors and onto the street where a town car with a driver was waiting. Jillian got up front and directed the driver where to go, while Lester got James and Lily's luggage squared away in the trunk. Lester motioned for James to meet him by the trunk, and James glided in that direction. It was clear Lester wanted to have a whispered moment with James, so he lowered his head to meet Lester's height allowing the trunk to serve as a cover from Lily for the private conversation. "She's beautiful." Lester spoke quietly into James' ear. James smiled a toothy grin.

"Yeah she is. She's incredible." Lester peered deeply into James' eyes. A quizitive look appeared on his face.

"You're not falling for this woman, are you? I've seen that look before and that look is dangerous for guys like us." James wiped the grin from his face and threw it up in the air.

"No, Les, we're just having a lot of fun. No need for concern. She's just a cool person who I enjoy spending time with. That's it!" Lester shook his head unconvinced.

"Why don't you let me sample the goods if she's just a cool person." James looked at Lester in disbelief.

"Are you serious?" James said with irritation in his voice.

"Yeah, I'm serious. Jil and I could definitely have some fun with that one. You shouldn't care if there ain't no feelings involved, right?" James waved him off.

"That'll be up to her, but I doubt she'll want to swing with y'all."

"Whatever you say." Lester closed the trunk and gave his friend one last look of concern. He threw his hands in the air in resignation and walked to the driver's side of the car.

The trio climbed into the back of the town car and closed the doors. Lily sat in the middle of the men, but she slid forward in the seat to give them a chance to chit chat. She looked out of the window as the car drove away from the airport. She watched as the scenery changed all around them. She'd never been to Jackson, Mississippi before, so she wanted to soak in the vibes from the city. The trip to downtown Jackson from the airport was less than a 20 minute drive, and mostly on the highway, but Lily felt like she'd reached a part of history as the streets and country life whizzed by. The guys talked the entire way, but Lily found herself in a daze. She was on a weekend getaway, out of town, and with a man she craved nightly. There was a peace that she felt there on the ride that no one could interrupt. Not even the singing grown little girl in the front seat belting out whatever popular song that was playing on the radio.

The driver pulled up in front of the door of a brick building with black awnings and the name *Johnny T's Bistro & Blues* written on one of them. The windows and doors had security bars as if the building was located in a bad neighborhood. Lily got out of the car and looked around. Some of the nearby buildings looked abandoned, but the church across the street looked well kept. It was a typical downtown that looked like it was in the rebuilding stages of revitalization. Jillian hopped out of the front seat and skipped towards the door. Lily looked at James as they exchanged a giggle. James walked over to Lily and put his arm around her shoulder. He whispered in her ear. "I'm happy to be here with you. Thank you for coming with me." Lily turned her face towards James' and kissed him on the lips to thank him in return for inviting her. Lester walked ahead to open the door of the restaurant. They were greeted with the sound of blues as they walked into the restaurant with James shifting his arm from around Lily's shoulders to around her waist. He hugged her from behind tightly and began to sway her back and forth. "Oh, we're definitely going to dance tonight." James whispered into Lily's ear.

"Here and back at the hotel, I hope." Lily replied. They followed Jillian and the hostess to their table. Lily saw they had plenty of seating in the restaurant. They passed a set of free-standing stairs on their way to their table and Lily could see there was an outdoor patio as well. The place seemed to have a welcoming feel, but it was the music that spoke to Lily's heart. The sound of the blues in the air made Lily feel sexy. Even though she'd been traveling all day and felt the stench of airline germs all over her, she still managed to find the excitement that permeated in the air.

James could tell that Lily liked the restaurant. He enjoyed watching her move to the beat of the music as she swayed back and forth in her chair. She was a person who never got to let loose. She always felt like critical eyes were watching her, but James could tell she was a different person out of town. She could be herself and relax, and that's exactly what James wanted for her. He wanted to see her real personality shine without worrying about who was going to judge her for it. The waiter came over to drop off a few menus but rushed away without truly greeting the table. James wasn't happy about that low level of service, but nothing was going to bother him about the evening. Not even a waiter who was too busy for them. Everyone grabbed a menu and studied it for a while. The group had the same idea. They figured they would only get one chance with the busy waiter, so they selected their entrees and libations all at once to maximize their opportunity. When he came back, everyone ordered their meals, and he disappeared once again.

James knew the music was coming from upstairs, so he grabbed Lily by the hand and escorted her towards the blues. Lily happily followed as she danced her way to the beat with each step. There was a small dance floor in the middle of the tables and high tops upstairs. No one was on it, but James didn't care. He wanted to work up a sweat and an appetite by connecting his body with Lily's. Some might call it dancing, but James wanted to grind. He pulled Lily in close to his body so she could feel every inch of him on her. He swayed her back and forth, never letting his pelvis leave hers. Lily closed her eyes to soak in the sensation. She could feel the blues covering each square inch of her body. It melted into her skin as she moved to and fro. Lily had never felt so sensual. She opened her eyes to see that other couples, including Lester and Jillian, had joined them on the dance floor. She looked at James who had been watching her the whole time with a devilish grin on his face. She knew and he knew that he had her in his physical grasp, but he also had her at his will. There was a spell that the blues had cast over them, and it made them feel hypnotized, powerless to the whim of the trumpet or the flutter of the bass. James could taste the sex in the air as he breathed in Lily's scent. She had begun to sweat from her body heat and from the thickness of the blues in the air. All James could think about was how alive he felt, and this was all because Lily said yes to their weekend in Jackson.

****

Lily held the hotel room key up to the lock pad of the door until she heard it beep and the green light flashed. She turned the handle and pushed on the heavy door. James followed her into the suite. He had clearly enjoyed too many Crown Peach Teas as he stumbled past her, the living and dining areas, and landed on the bed with a *plop*. He remained there face down for a second while he gathered himself. Lily heard a tap on the door. She walked over to the door and looked through the peephole. It was Lester and Jillian standing there. Lily opened the door and saw Lester had brought their luggage upstairs. He and Jillian rolled the bags past Lily and into the room. They clearly had their sober wits about them, yet James and Lily felt the sting of an alcohol buzz on their heads. Lester reached in his pocket and pulled out two blindfolds. "Here." Lester demanded as he extended his arm for Lily to take the items out of his hand. "If this guy ever sobers up and you two want to have some real fun, the party will be in room 1117." Lily looked at the blindfolds in her hand and then back at Lester.

"What kind of party are we talking about?" Lily asked with curious hesitation.

"James knows. He'll fill you in." Lester then took Lily by the hand and kissed it gentlemanly, then he and Jillian walked towards the door. "That's room 1117." Lester repeated as he walked out. The sound of the door slamming shut roused James.

"Hey babe. How long was I out?" He sat up on the edge of the bed and rubbed his head.

"Just a few minutes. Long enough for us to get a strange invite to the 'real fun' by Lester and Jillian." Lily held up air quotes as she sarcastically relayed Lester's message. "He said you would know what that meant." James continued to rub his head, but this time he was trying to get a grasp of what Lily was saying.

"What do you mean?" James asked

"Lester gave me these blindfolds and told us to come up to 1117. What in the freaky hell did you volunteer us for?" Lily was clearly anxious about every possible scenario that was playing out in her mind. She'd always been a sexual free spirit, but only with her immediate partner. The thought of being blinded, naked, and in a new city with strangers terrified her. James could clearly see her angst and rushed over to comfort her.

"Listen, we don't have to go up there. Why don't we put on a movie and just chill here? I came here to be with you and to give the most powerful sermon at the conference tomorrow night. That's all." James escorted Lily to the bed and sat her down. "Let me try to explain. See, Lester was married to Maria for almost 40 years. They were high school sweethearts. Once he got a job working in a mill, and could support a family, he married the love of his life. Maria was his everything. She was the type of woman who kept a tidy household, entertained friends and family with her outgoing personality, and kept him satisfied in the bedroom. Then, she went to work to support the family so he could focus on going to seminary. She didn't want to be a pastor's wife, but she loved Lester. So, she always did what she had to do for him and for the family. Maria passed away about two years ago. Ever since then, Lester hasn't been the same. It's like he's trying to see different women to piece together the one woman that was Maria. And in his Frankenstein efforts, he's pushing the envelope farther and farther to regain the feeling that he'll never get again from his wife. Obviously, this all has to be behind closed doors because he's a respected pastor around these parts, but it's clear he's spiraling. I think that's another reason why I wanted to come here. I wanted to lay eyes on my friend and see if there was anything I could do to help. The problem is that most people don't check on their strong friends. They assume they'll be all right because they're strong. But who's really there for them when they need the strength? You can't tell your members that you're hurting and don't want to get out of bed most days. A pastor's role is to give, give, give. People take so much from us that they forget to pour back into the empty jar that just quenched their thirst. They leave satisfied while our mental resources are drained. I know this all seems strange to you right now, but trust me, there's a reason why we are how we are. We are human. Lester is being a human in his grief."

Lily sat back on the headboard as she thought about what James had told her. She understood now that Lester, as old as he is now, wasn't being himself. That totally explained the younger woman and whatever was happening in room 1117. Although she understood, it didn't mean she had to participate in it. James joined Lily on the bed at the headrest. He spooned close to her body and held her tightly. Lily pushed her bottom back to fit into what little space was between them. "I'm glad I'm here with you." Lily said, as the corners of her mouth rose. "It feels good to be with someone so caring and warm. You're a good man, James." James squeezed Lily a little tighter. Lily was tired, but she wanted to make love to James. She could feel that James was excited to be holding her, but it wasn't the right time to make a move. Lily reached over to the nightstand and grabbed the television remote. She turned on the television and found a movie channel. She drifted to sleep before even seeing the plot.

It couldn't have been more than a couple hours later when Lily heard the sound of James' phone ringing. She didn't bother to open her eyes when James stopped holding her and took his phone to the bathroom because she began drifting back to sleep. The conversation was brief and he returned to the spooning position. Seconds later, Lily felt James' luscious kisses on her neck. She was tired from traveling and from dancing to the blues, but there was something about James that made her moisture level rise immediately. Wrapped around her, his strong hands slid up her body to meet his kisses on her neck. Lily loved when he pulled her close. It made her feel like she was in the presence of a real man, which reminded her that she enjoyed being powerless in the bedroom. James turned Lily to face him and kissed her lips passionately. It took her breath away because of the unexpected heat behind his kiss. Just minutes ago, she was in a deep sleep and now this man was in full *I want you* mode. Lily closed her eyes and gave in as James pulled her into is masculine chest. She was breathing his air as her body began to open up with excitement. Just then, James let her go and slightly pushed her away. Again, a total surprise as Lily was ready to mount his love in what was sure to be an orgasmic experience. But James had other plans in mind. He grabbed one of the blindfolds that Lester had given them and placed it over Lily's eyes. This was a first for Lily, but she was fully invested in the idea of how heightened her other senses would be. Lily licked her lips in excitement.

"You like that, huh?" James asked as he ensured the blindfold was snug. Lily nodded in agreement as she licked her lips again. It wasn't just the blindfold that James planned for Lily. He retrieved a necktie from his suitcase and walked back to Lily. "Don't be afraid," he whispered as he grabbed both of her hands.

A wave of curiosity hovered over Lily, but she was never afraid with James. She enjoyed his sexual experience and willingness to get to know her body. He cared for every inch of her, down to her toenails. How could she be afraid? James tied her hands with the tie. It was a little tight, but Lily knew it was all a part of whatever plan James had to please her. She could feel his hands start to undress her from the waist down. Lily attempted to reach out to James but her hands were bound. James saw this attempt and raised her hands above her head. He slid her body back to the headrest of the bed and connected the necktie to the reading lamp above the headrest. Lily couldn't see or make use of her hands. The erotic pleasure vibrated throughout her body. She had never been so pleasantly terrified and turned on at the same time. She loved how kinky this hotel room was feeling.

He finished undressing Lily from the waist down. She could hear James' feet step back, presumably to admire his work, and waited for him to touch her again. And she waited. Curious, Lily called out to James. "Papi, ¿estás aquí?" No one answered. Just then, Lily heard the door open and swing closed. A strange feeling began to come over her. Before, she felt a good terror. The feeling of heightened anticipation of James' manly touch or maybe his lips taking advantage of her vulnerable state. But this feeling wasn't that. It was more like a feeling of actual fear. This wasn't something she'd ever experienced before. She knew James would never put her in a position to be scared on purpose, so she rationalized in her mind that maybe he had gone for condoms but wanted to keep up the silent charade. It may have felt like forever, but a few moments later, Lily could hear the lock pad unlock and the door open again. "No me jodas, papi. Ya sabes que estoy lista para…" Lily waited for a response but James was still playing the silent game. She heard his feet approach and began to feel the wave of fear leave her body and a sense of pleasure return. Her sense of confidence returned, and she knew how much men loved to hear her speak the only Spanish she knew, which was all bedroom talk. Hell, she was in a new city, in a strange hotel room, blindfolded, and bound to the bed. If this wasn't the time to break out her Carmen persona, then she couldn't think of a better time. She could only presume that James was still admiring his handy work and that's why he was so quiet and not touching her, but she decided to be patient and let this play out how she was hoping in her mind it would.

"Do you trust me?" James finally whispered.

"Si, papi. Confio en ti." Lily replied with lust in her voice. James walked up and cupped Lily's face with his hands. He kissed her sweetly.

"Be good to them." He said as he turned and walked away. Lily froze. She heard three sets of footsteps this time. One set was clearly walking away and the others walking towards her. Just then, the door opened and closed just as quickly. It occurred to Lily at that moment that she was alone in the room with a strange man or men. She assumed one was Lester, but she couldn't be sure. Lily's terror turned to rage. Granted, the entire nature of their relationship was based on sex, but what would make James think he could share her with other people? Why would he think that she would be ok with sharing her body with people she didn't know. She was furious. Her body began to tremble ferociously when she felt a soft touch on her upper thigh. The hand was delicate and gentle like a woman. At this point it was no surprise that Jillian and Lester were her two strangers. Jillian's hands ran up her in a straight line to her breasts. She leaned down and French kissed Lily's left nipple. Lily could smell Jillian's perfume and it made her stomach sick. This whole experience was sickening, but Lily was too disgusted to move or say a word. It was obvious what was happening, so when Lester opened her legs, pulled her bottom to the edge of the bed, and proceeded to insert his short, stubby dick into her sacred place, Lily didn't bother to fake like she was ok with this violation. Lester pounded away in a short and heavy hunch. He had a stomach that was obviously a baby protected by beer flavored amniotic fluid. Of course, he wasn't concerned with pleasing her. He wasn't concerned with who she was or her values. Thankfully, he was concerned with both of their safety because he had the decency to wear a condom, but he was truly there to get off.

For what felt like the longest five minutes of her life, Lily was rabbit-like humped at the edge of the bed. Lester's voice was heavy as he outwardly moaned with pleasure. He was clearly enjoying his experience. She could feel her cooch drying up by the second, which made her experience not only violating, but painful. Lily sensed Lester was close to being done as his knees began to weaken and his humps became more intense. He finally exploded in a loud, convulsing motion as if the orgasm had taken all life and strength out of his body. He removed his still quivering member and slowly slumped his large body to the floor. In an unexpected move, he put his face between Lily's legs and started flicking his tongue uncontrollably at Lily's whole vagina with untrained and sloppy motions. He clearly wasn't aiming for any one part because he was making a spitty mess between her legs. Lily pulled away defiantly and retreated towards the headboard. Getting the message, Lester stood up and she could hear footsteps backing away.

Then, Lily felt Jillian's touch again. This time, it was on her foot. Jillian sat on the bed at Lily's feet and kissed her knee. It was a kiss that felt understanding. A kiss that felt empathetic. She knew Lily didn't enjoy Lester's untamed dick, but she knew how to make her feel better for at least a moment. She kissed Lily's other knee and used her nose to separate Lily's legs. She gently kissed each inner thigh as she used her hands to slide down the outer thighs. Jillian wanted Lily to know that she cared about *her* pleasure at that moment. Lily appreciated the gesture even though the thought was just as twisted and off putting as the fact that she was in the room in the first place. Jillian used the same French kiss on Lily's clitoris to send shock waves throughout her body. It was clear Jillian was no stranger to the female form. She gave Lily instant pleasure as she continued to kiss and gently tug on the places she knew Lily would love. Lily gave into the pleasure. Hell, she deserved to feel good after what James and Lester just put her through. Although conflicted between torment and ecstasy, Lily allowed herself to climax and sit in her orgasm while Jillian removed herself from the bed.

In the faint distance, Lily heard what sounded like a high five. *What the fuck? Was someone else in the room? Did James stay to watch? Was this another stranger that witnessed Lily's defiant consent? Or was it Lester congratulating Jillian for what he couldn't do?* "I need everyone to leave." Lily whispered firmly. She slid all the way back to the headboard again and removed her hands from the light fixture. It took her a second, but she was able to untie herself and remove the blindfold. She blinked her eyes to regain her sight, hoping to catch a glimpse of the people in her room, but the door was closing when she regained her vision. She thought to herself that it was better that she didn't know. At that point, still feeling her blood boiling inside of her body, she didn't want to know. She grabbed her suitcase and headed towards the bathroom. She immediately made a b-line for the shower and turned it on to the hottest setting. She got in the shower and sat down against the back wall. The tears began to unexpectedly flow down her cheeks in silent rage. There wasn't a need for her to sob, the running water made all the noise she or anyone else needed to hear.

The next morning, Lily found herself in bed alone. She didn't know if James had come back to the room or if he had actually slept in the bed next to her. Lily blinked her eyes open to see James sitting at the dining room table, reading his tablet. Lily was usually an early riser too, but the events from the previous day had made her tired both physically and emotionally. She sat up in the bed to get a clearer look at him. James was wearing sweat-stained workout clothes and was glistening from his post-workout sweat.

She couldn't bring herself to speak to him just yet, so she changed into her workout clothes right next to her bag and headed towards the door. James looked up from his tablet to see that Lily was dressed and leaving. He looked like he was about to speak, but just then, his cell phone rang. She watched as he looked at the screen ID. It was clearly Alice or one of the kids calling. He answered with a joyful hello as Lily grabbed the room key off of the table next to the door and tiptoed out, being sure to close the door gently. Once out safe in the hallway, Lily walked towards the elevator. She couldn't believe the predicament she'd gotten herself into. Her feelings were bittersweet. She was feeling confused and guilty at the same time. A run always cleared her head, so she couldn't wait to tuck all her feelings into a tight little bow and just run on the treadmill. She pressed the elevator down button and waited patiently for the door to open. The doors slowly opened to reveal Jillian, still wearing her clothes from the night before, kissing a man that clearly wasn't Lester. Jillian pushed the man back and adjusted her already disheveled clothes. Lily looked at Jillian's face with her mascara smeared and Joker-esk lipstick stained face and couldn't help but frown at the two-fold walk of shame. "Good morning." Lily greeted with a disgusted face as she entered the elevator. Although it was already illuminated, Lily pushed the L for lobby button again, pleading with the elevator doors to close quickly.

"Good morning," the man greeted. Jillian stayed silent in the corner of the elevator, clearly embarrassed by the surprise encounter. Lily looked at her watch. It was a little after 7:00 a.m. Surely Jillian figured no one would be awake to catch her creeping out this early in the morning with whoever this mystery man was, but Lily didn't particularly care what Jillian was doing. After hearing about Maria and the monstrosity of the night before, Lily couldn't have cared less about what Jillian, or any other woman was doing with or to Lester. The elevator arrived at the lobby level, and everyone quietly exited without a word. Lily made her way through the lobby towards the workout room. She found it quickly and used her room key to get into the door. There was a stack of hand towels at the entrance, so Lily grabbed one and quickly located a vacant treadmill at the back of the room. She aligned her settings and began to walk as her warm-up.

Lily regretted not bringing her headphones. She could usually get on the treadmill and let Bruno Mars take her to where she needed to go. Some days she needed to catch a grenade and others she needed the silk to make her feel sexy. Either way, Bruno had just the vibe she needed to keep her focused on her run. But today, she had the unfortunate luck to be alone with her own thoughts on her run. As the warm-up period expired, her treadmill took her to her usual, fast-paced jog. Lily tried not to think about James. Her thoughts started with the office. She began to think about if the new medical assistant had set the office phones to away mode so the on-call doctor could receive emergency calls. "No work, Lily." She said to herself aloud. She then began to think about getting a dog. Maybe she was lonely. A furry companion would be just what she needed to not feel forlorn and leave this married man alone. *Nope. Too much like having a baby.* She thought to herself. It wasn't that Lily didn't want kids, she loved kids. It was that she also enjoyed sleeping in and moving on a whim. At this point in her life, she'd rather be focused on finding a husband of her own and not being a responsible pet owner.

Her thoughts were making her run seem longer. She needed the right distraction to get out of her own head. She definitely didn't want to think about the night before. Lately, during her runs, she would think about all the nasty things she wanted to do with James, but that just took her back to the thought of James. This run wasn't about him. It was about her. She scolded herself for thinking about him all the time. She cranked up the speed in anger. Why couldn't she manage to have a moment to herself without thinking of this man? This man who clearly doesn't care anything about her. Was she that dickmatized that she couldn't find an original thought. The sex was top notch, but it had only happened a handful of times and at the same small hotel outside of town. She was enraged at how much mental real estate she was allowing James to take up. By now, she was in a full sprint on the treadmill.

Lily heard the door to the gym open and close. She looked down at the timer on her machine and saw that 25 minutes had elapsed. She adjusted her settings to slow down to cool-down mode. "Don't let me slow you down." Lily turned around to see James standing behind her with a wide grin on his face. Her heart and her anger still pumping, she hopped off the machine and walked aggressively towards James. His expression quickly changed as he saw the rage in her eyes. He braced himself for her to hit him, but he received the opposite. Lily landed a passionate kiss on his lips. James scooped her into his arms and reciprocated her intensity. He was a bit confused and aroused at the same time. Lily pulled back suddenly.

"Let's go." She demanded, as she walked towards the door. James willingly followed. Lily pushed the door open forcefully and continued walking. James slid through the narrow opening before the door bounced back to slam shut. Again, James was confused, but totally open to see where this scene was leading. Lily made a b-line towards the elevators. She pushed the elevator up button and waited with her arms folded. She didn't look back to even see if James had followed her. She knew he was there behind her, because, with how she was feeling right now, he had better been behind her. The elevator doors opened, and Lily and James got on. Another couple tried to enter the elevator, but Lily blocked their way. "We just finished working out. It's going to be pretty smelly in here. You may want to catch the next one." The man grabbed his woman by the hand and pulled her back. He couldn't tell if Lily was being serious or not, but the intense look on her face gave him enough pause to know not to get on the elevator. The door closed and Lily turned to a shocked James. She instinctively smiled at his unexpecting terror. Hell, that's what she felt last night. She turned to the elevator and pressed the stop button. The elevator came to a screeching halt between floors. "We have about 10 minutes before the manager calls into the elevator to see if there's a problem. You think you can get the job done before then?" James looked puzzled.

"Job?" Lily pushed James back to the elevator railing and kissed him with all the sensation she had in her mouth. James grabbed her by the shoulder and pushed her back. "Oh that job?" He said to her as he turned her around and pulled her pants and panties down. Lily put her hands on the elevator wall to brace herself. James pulled down his pants to reveal his engorged eggplant and gently, yet firmly, slid into the cavity of Lily's body as they both groaned with pleasure. Maybe it was the adrenaline or possibly perspective. Lily was clearly an object to James. If she was going to continue or not continue this relationship, then she had to take away his power. She needed to be in control of the when and with whom she gave her body. She had to remind herself, this is a married pastor whose sole purpose was one thing, her pleasure. That's the only way this arrangement was ever going to be mutually fun, was if she turned the tables and demanded a portion of the control. This elevator and this moment was a symbol of her imposing her will. And if he wasn't going to get on board, then she was going to get off the ride.

James had to go ahead to the church in preparation for his sermon, so Lily stayed behind to read an article in a medical journal. Lester's driver had already dropped the guys off, so he was able to circle back around to pick up Lily. She was waiting at the entrance to the hotel when he pulled up. He greeted her with a warm smile as he exited the town car and walked around the front to the passenger side. He opened Lily's door and allowed her full entry into the front seat before closing the door. "Thank you." Lily replied politely to the gesture. Lily didn't like the idea of riding around with a perfect stranger, especially knowing that James didn't have a problem putting her in harm's way, but she didn't get the sense that this man would harm her, so she shook off the thought. The driver walked around to the driver's side door, but before he could open it, a driver sped through the guest drop off lane, almost hitting him. He yelled some obscenities the driver's way before getting in the car.

"They almost made me cuss." The driver exclaimed as he closed the door.

"Almost?" Lily asked with a smile. They both had a hearty laugh. The driver took off down the road. Lily looked out the window and admired the historical city. Yes, it looked rather run down, but she could feel the love pouring out of each historical landmark. They made their way to the church in mostly silence. Lily could tell the driver was dying to talk to her, but she wasn't really in the mood for conversation. She finally broke the silence. "I'm sorry. I didn't catch your name."

"Douglas." The driver replied quickly. "And you're Lily. What a pretty name." Lily smiled shyly. "How do you know Pastor J?" Lily dreaded that question from the moment she entered the car. How should she answer that question? The truth wasn't exactly the most savory of explanations. But she was on the way to church, so she couldn't tell a lie. It was a truly complicated question.

"We work together on the after school program at the church." That was the best answer. It was the truth, it explained why she would be in Jackson, possibly on church business, and it was enough information that he wouldn't need to ask a follow up question. Lily could hear the driver talking, but she was overpowered by her own thoughts again. Maybe the run didn't exactly clear her head. Maybe the sex in the elevator wasn't exactly what she needed to take back her power. Here she was, sitting in the car with a stranger, and trying not to feel guilty about being out of town with a married man while trying not to reveal that she'd been having an affair with him for several months.

The previous day felt too uncomfortable for her and she was torn. If she let her guard down, she could find herself falling in love with James. He was in fact the perfect man for her. He was just as handsome as he was personable, he loved to travel, he could dance, and the sex was dynamite. They could talk for hours if they had the time. On Sundays, she could get lost in his sermons because he had a way with words that could engage your soul as well as your mind. But Lily knew the rules. She knew love wasn't a word that was supposed to be in their vocabulary. But, it felt so right in her soul to want to spend more and more time with him. He was her perfect equal. On the other hand, this is the same man that shared her physically with other people. How could she be ok with the two sides of the same coin? Lily knew a decision couldn't be made in that moment, but she knew she had to get back to familiar territory. "Can we please make a route change?" Lily interrupted the driver, who was clearly speaking to someone who wasn't listening. He looked at her puzzled. "I'm sorry, I'm not feeling so well. I think I should go back to the hotel and lay down."

"Of course." He replied. Still confused, he made a U-turn at the traffic light to head back to the hotel. Lily had no intention of lying down. She was going to take a rideshare to the airport and go home. She didn't care what it cost, she didn't care how late she would get in, but she knew she had to get back to familiar territory. The luster of this affair was wearing off and becoming too real. She'd always promised herself that she'd get out of this messy situation when it stopped being fun. The confusion swirling in her head wasn't fun. It was time to get the heck out of Dodge City and back to where she could be the Marshall, deputy, saloon owner, and doctor of her town called home. She pulled out her cell phone and sent James a text message. "I can't." And quickly put her phone on Do Not Disturb mode.

Andrea Furlow

The Competition

James stood up when it was time for his row to exit the plane, but he felt ill. There was a churning in his stomach that could only be caused by guilt. He knew he had let things go too far with Lily, but that was the only way he knew how to distance himself from getting too close to her. He was developing feelings for this woman, and that was never the plan. James remembered how he got rid of a woman back in his playing days. He knew that once she was someone else's conquest, then she could never be his. It was an immediate divestment that he grew to rely on. But this time was different. He felt guilty. He felt like he was going to vomit with shame and embarrassment. He felt out of control, which wasn't like him. As he walked towards the baggage claim, he looked down at his phone hoping to see a missed call or text message from Lily, but all he saw were text messages with requests from his kids and a note from Alice of where to meet her in the pickup area. He was hoping that a glance at Alice's lovely face would make him refocus his mind on her and the boys, and it did. As soon as he walked out the door, and saw the giant smile on Alice's face, he couldn't help but feel a sense of peace. Alice had always been his peace. She worked every time.

James lifted the rear gate and threw his bag in the back. He walked to the driver's side and opened Alice's door. He took her by the hands and pulled her out of the car. He needed to embrace her full body and allow her to grip his back as she always did. James inhaled her full essence. She had on a new perfume. It wasn't pleasant to his nose, but he just kept holding onto her until all his cares and memories from the weekend had passed.

Alice tried to pull away but was met with resistance. "Love, are you ok?" Alice inquired.

"I'm fine. I just missed you, that's all." James let go of Alice and kissed her sweetly on the forehead. "Let's get out of here." Alice walked around to the passenger side of the car and let herself in. James climbed into the driver's seat and adjusted the settings.

"I know you'll want to get to the church to check on things, but do you want to grab some lunch first?" Alice asked. James could feel his stomach grumbling, but he couldn't tell if it was still turning from not knowing if Lily was ok or if it was actual hunger. He shrugged, which indicated to Alice that it was her choice if they stopped or not. "Let's grab a sandwich from the diner across the street and we can decide if we'll eat at the bar or take it to go."

"That's fine." James drove quickly out of the airport exit and towards the highway. He let his mind wander as Alice tried to make small talk. He wasn't in the mood to chat, but he also knew that Alice was. He tried his best to be present in the moment, but the powers of her hug were quickly wearing off as he got closer to the church. He knew Lily would be there. He knew she would never default on her obligation to the children, even if she felt some kind of way about what happened in Jackson.

James pulled into the diner parking lot, but he could see Lily's car in the church lot. He wasn't ready to face her, but it was time. "Honey, can you please grab me my usual salad? I'm just going to take it to go and eat in my office as I work on my lesson for Wednesday's Bible study. I've got a new series in mind, and I don't want to lose the thought." Alice smiled and nodded in agreement. She got out of the car and walked towards the diner. James tossed her the keys so she could drive over to the church lot when she was done getting the food. James began his slow walk towards the church. He didn't know if he'd be greeted with smiles or disappointment, but it was time to take that chance. The sun made an appearance to break the cold hair. It felt good on James' face, but it was too bright not to use his hand to shade his eyes. He looked both ways before crossing the street towards the church. He could hear laughing from afar, which sounded familiar. As he approached, he could see Lily with her back turned and a strange man standing in front of her. She had her hand flirtatiously placed on his chest as she leaned into him and laughed. It was intimate, and James was jealous as hell. He picked up the pace and trotted across the street to see who this man was.

As he approached, James' sightline of this man got better. He was very tall and very tan, with shoulder-length hair. His hair was twisted in a way that looked like he had just undone a ponytail. He towered over Lily in a way that felt intimidating. It felt as if this man was posturing to say *you're going to be my woman*. That made James want to get over there quicker to protect what was his. The man looked up at James and gave him a sly smile.

"This must be him." The man said in a slightly southern accent, gesturing towards James. Lily turned towards the man's gaze with her teeth leading the charge. There was a smile on her face as her hair floated in the wind and landed perfectly on her back. Her energy was on 1000 and yet her flawless appearance was never disturbed by her enthusiasm for the conversation.

"That is him. Pastor J, please meet Dr. Eric Rollins. He's the dentist I was telling you about. He'll be here once a month to check on the dental health of the kids in our church and community. He's from Gaffney, South Carolina, which is about an hour from here, but he's so graciously offered to drive here every month to check on our kiddos." Lily turned to look at Eric in admiration. Eric returned her affection with a huge smile and a wink.

"Nice to meet you." Eric said in his low, baritone voice as he extended his hand to James to shake. James was taken aback by Eric's presence. He was an overtly large man. James could see he was muscular through his scrubs and white coat. Not to mention he was exotic and handsome. James shook his hand firmly to establish his presence, but it was clear who the real winner of the moment was.

"Nice to meet you, too. We're blessed to have you." James turned his attention to Lily. "Dr. Lily, may I have a word with you?" Lily went to reply but was interrupted by Alice who was flinging a bag of food in James' direction.

"My my my, Dr. Lily. Who do we have here?" Alice stepped in between Lily and James to extend her hand to greet Eric. "I'm Alice."

"Don't be disrespectful." James mumbled under his breath.

"The pleasure is all mine." Eric replied. "I followed your entire career, and I have to say, I'm a huge fan. There aren't many athletes, male or female, who could do what you did. You're so amazing."

"Well thank you kindly, sir." Alice's poor attempt at a southern accent was amusing to all. She shook Eric's hand and then stepped back behind James. She rubbed his back in a loving way. It was obvious to her that the taller, more handsome man was intimidating to James. Her back rub was to reassure him that he was her man no matter what.

James looked at Lily who hadn't taken her eyes off of Eric. "Dr. Lily?" He reminded her.

"Pastor, I'm going to get Dr. Eric set up in the auxiliary room. Do you mind if I meet you back in your office later?" Lily didn't wait for an answer. She grabbed Eric by the arm and escorted him towards the main building of the church.

James' blood was boiling. It wasn't that she was interested in someone else. It was the fact that she fucked him and left him in Jackson just the day before and yet this other man had piqued her interest so quickly. Alice continued to stand behind James. She admired the couple as they walked away. "What a lovely couple." She remarked.

"They're not a couple." James sniped. Alice took her eyes off of Lily and Eric to look at James and study his face.

"If I didn't know any better, I would say you're jealous, Pastor." Alice chuckled to herself. James immediately became defensive.

"I'm not jealous. I just don't think we should go marrying off people who just met." Alice grabbed James by the head, lowered it, and kissed his crown.

"I love you, James. I'm going to the outlets to shop and meet a friend. I'll be home to pick up the boys from practice. Want anything special for dinner?" James waved Alice off and walked towards the church. "Meatloaf and mashed potatoes it is." Alice announced, then retrieved her keys from her pocket and walked towards her car. "Dinner is at 7." She called over her shoulder as she opened the car door and climbed in.

James was red with anger. He knew he couldn't go into the building and see the two of them all starry-eyed. He decided to turn back towards the church office. The cold air hit his face as he walked into the shade of the building. James made his way up the stairs towards the church office door. His brain was swirling, but he needed some advice. He needed to know if he had let his guard down too far and now it might be too late to pull it back up. He pulled his cell phone out of his pocket and thumbed through the contacts until he found Dr. Michaels' phone number. James contemplated what he would say. It had been months since they'd last spoken. James knew he was only supposed to kill his curiosity with Lily. He wasn't supposed to develop feelings for her. He needed another thought to swirl in his brain. Maybe a voice of reason would cast out the loud sound of his sanity crashing all around him. He pressed Dr. Michaels' name, and the phone began to dial. "Dr. Michaels' office," an unfamiliar female voice answered.

"Good morning, or rather, good afternoon. I'd like to speak to Dr. Michaels. This is. . ."

"Yes, James. I'll be happy to patch you in. One moment please." James was taken aback. *Where was Dr. Michaels' no good soon to be son in law? How did this lady know my name? And, was Dr. Michaels expecting my call?* Dr. Michaels came onto the line fairly quickly.

"Hello James. It's been a long time. How are you?" James took a deep breath. "That bad, huh?" Dr. Michaels responded for him.

"I'm doing ok, doc. Life had been going well up until this past weekend. Remember I told you about a woman the last time we spoke. Well, I think I may have let things get a little out of hand, and now I think I have feelings for her. And before you say anything about how I messed up, let me be the first to admit it. I messed up." James took another deep breath, which allowed Dr. Michaels to interject.

"James, there's clearly a story here. Why don't you tell me what happened this past weekend and let me decide if I feel some type of way about it. Remember, there's no judgment on my part. I'm only here to listen and guide you in the right direction. That's all." James took a sigh of relief and began.

"Over the last few months, I've been seeing Lily at our usual motel out of town. We have sex, maybe a meal, and we go about our business. I see her once a week during daylight hours at the church when she volunteers, and then I see her every Sunday for service. Well lately, I found myself seeking out her face in the crowd. My sermons get even more passionate when I finally see her. She could be in the balcony, in the back corner, or on the front row. I seek and find her every week. That wasn't supposed to happen. It's not just the sex with her. It's intimate. I've tried to compartmentalize our relationship, but somehow, she's broken into my spirit. I think about her all the time. It's really distracting. So anyway, this past weekend, we took our relationship to the next level. I invited her to Jackson, Mississippi with me. I was having a conference, and I thought it would be nice to have a change of scenery. We had a great dinner the first night. We came back to the room and fell asleep while watching a movie. In the middle of the night, my buddy called me and asked if he and his girlfriend could swing with me and Lily. I told him no because I didn't think it was appropriate at the time, but he said something that made me think. He asked if I loved her or was, she just an itch that needed to be scratched. At that moment, I didn't think I was falling in love with her, and I had to be sure I could let her go at a moment's notice, if necessary. So, I invited him and his girlfriend into our bed." James put his hand on top of his head in grief. His breath began to leave his throat and his eyes began to tear. He looked around the parking lot to ensure no one could see his sudden rush of emotion. Before he could continue, he walked around to the side of the church office and propped himself up against the building. That was going to be the only way he could guarantee he wouldn't pass out. He continued. "I couldn't stay to watch. I just left before I could see him touch her." Dr. Michaels needed some clarity, so he waited for a natural pause to insert his question.

"I'm not judging you, but I want to ask a clarifying question. Was this a test for you to see if you really cared about this woman or were you appeasing the pleasures of your friend? I want to be clear about your intentions before I respond to what you've said so far."

"I guess it was a bit of both." James responded. "I think mostly to gauge my feelings." James shook his head and sat all the way down on the cold ground next to the building. Phone in one hand and head in his other, James waited for Dr. Michaels to hit him with a hard dose of reality.

"James, I can sense this makes you a bit emotional. I can hear it in your voice. So I'll just respond to what you've told me and then we can dive deeper into how you want to move forward in a minute. First, thank you for sharing this with me. It's hard to seek advice after a decision has been made, and you knew my feedback wasn't going to be favorable, so I appreciate your bravery in calling me. Second, let me say that I'm a little disappointed in how you've treated this woman. I don't know the details of how things went down in the bedroom, but you left her unprotected and exposed to the sexual whim of people she didn't know or go there to see. You made her vulnerable in a way that she would have never exposed herself. And, I'm positive it was without her consent. Even if you didn't have feelings for her, why would you put any woman in that position? Now that's not a question we're going to answer just yet. But I want you to think about it as we continue. Lastly, I want you to think about how you want to move forward. Because, at this point, you're beyond the simple physical affair that we talked about a few months ago. It has now become emotional. We need to dive deeper into what has and will happen."

"James?" A voice called. James looked up to see Lily was standing over him.

"Doc, I have to call you back." James said as he hung up the phone without waiting for a reply. "Lily. I, um, I need to talk to you." James wiped his eyes and stood to his feet. He put his phone in his pocket as he approached Lily."

"No, James, we don't need to talk. That's what I was coming to tell you." She put out her hand at chest level to stop James from getting into her personal space. He ran directly into the palm of her hand and used his strength to pull her closer. Lily struggled back a little, but James managed to wrap both of his arms around her and draw her close.

"I'm so sorry, baby. I've been kicking myself all night and day. I don't know what I was thinking. Maybe I wasn't thinking. All I know is I *need* you to forgive me." Lily continued to struggle as James tried to hold on.

"Everything all right out here?" Eric asked, as he quickly approached the still flailing Lily. James let her go, but Lily still pushed James in the chest as a form of protest and disgust.

"Everything is fine, Eric." Lily gave James a stare of death as her eyes filled with rage and tears. "Pastor just found out some bad news and he needs a minute to process what he's feeling. We all handle loss differently. Let's go to lunch like we planned and give Pastor some space to grieve." Lily finally broke contact with James and blinked her tears away. She turned and smiled at Eric, who was still puzzled. She reached out her hand for him to hold. "Yes. Let's eat. I'm hungry." Eric grabbed her hand and looked at a stunned James still standing in place. He had the feeling he'd walked into something more, but he wanted to respect Lily's wishes.

"Sure. Let's go. Do you mind if I drive? We can come back and get your car later."

"That would be nice. Thank you." Lily and Eric walked towards his black sedan, and he let her into the passenger side. He closed the door and took one last look at James before he got into the drivers' seat and drove off.

****

James let the shower water hit his head and rush down his body. It had been weeks since he'd spoken to Lily. She hadn't been to the church in several Sundays, she missed her turn to volunteer with the children, and she clearly blocked the calls and text messages from his phone number. All he could do was live through her eyes on social media. It was obvious that she and Eric had begun to date more seriously. There were hundreds of pictures of the two of them in and out of town. James watched the video of Eric effortlessly tossing Lily over a 6-foot fence so they could take selfies with "The Peach" what felt like a million times. She looked so happy being outside and able to share her joy with the world. It was miles better than their secret meet ups in the back of the motel out of town. The smile on her face said it all, and it made James feel so helpless. It was as if their time together never happened. He realized pretty early on that he'd fallen for Lily. It wasn't intentional, but it never was in these situations.

"Honey?" Alice's voice called from the bathroom door. "I'm headed out for the day. Can I bring you back anything?"

"No, my love, I'll see you later." James called from underneath the running water. He knew Alice could tell he was different, and he felt bad that he was being distant from her. It's just that the thoughts in his head for Lily were constantly running on a treadmill in his mind. They were going nowhere but wouldn't stop long enough for him to get off. Yeah, of course he could hit the emergency stop button if he wanted, but then he wouldn't be connected to Lily at all.

James could hear his phone ringing across the bathroom, but he had no desire to go get it. It was probably Dr. Michaels calling back again. He'd been avoiding the doctor's call ever since it had ended so abruptly at the church the day he got back from Jackson. James knew the doctor was concerned, but he also didn't need to beat himself up more than he already did. It was clear that the shower was doing more harm than good, so he turned the water off and opened the shower door. He let the cool air rush in and hit his body. He stood there for another minute before he got out to retrieve his towel. What James didn't want to think about was his next steps. Would he tell Alice? Would he try to reconcile with Lily? Would he just pretend that nothing happened and move on? So many unnecessary decisions needed to be made now and all because he gave into the overwhelming feeling of attraction and excitement of seeing Lily.

James knew he couldn't keep spiraling. He wrapped the towel around his waist and went to look for his phone. He'd placed it on the countertop next to the sink, which was clear across the bathroom. He had to backtrack the direction his body was already traveling in. As he turned to step in the opposite direction, he slipped on a pool of water that collected beyond the bathmat. Being a former athlete, James knew to put his arm out to brace himself for the fall. What he didn't anticipate was how hard he'd fall on his elbow. The pain that rocketed through his arm and all the way to his brain was alarming. James knew this wasn't going to be good. He sat on the floor naked and cradling his right arm. He knew he didn't want to call Alice and ruin her day just yet. He decided to call Saul. Saul could come over and help him get dressed and take him to the urgent care facility down the street. This way, he could spare Alice, get fixed up, and have a session to vent about Lily. He hadn't told anyone about Lily, but Saul was a trusted friend. He would never tell anyone, and that's exactly what James needed - a friend.

It was going to be a challenge for James to roll his way over to his phone. The pain that was beginning to permeate throughout this body was becoming unbearable. He'd had injuries during his playing days, but those were many years ago. He couldn't remember the feeling of pain anywhere other than his heart, and honestly his pride too. James rolled himself onto his left side and used his left elbow and knee to get into a kneeling position. He was then able to stand to his feet from there. He walked over to the sink to get his phone. He saw the slew of missed calls and text messages, but his mission was to get Saul on the line. He found Saul's name in his contacts and pressed it with purpose.

"Hel - um hello. James? I mean, Pastor? Is that you?" Saul was clearly out of breath. It sounded like he was running or working out.

"Hey man. Did I catch you at a bad time?" James inquired

"No sir. I was, um, working up a sweat. I'm finished now. What's going on?"

"Sorry to bother you, man, but I had a little accident at home."

"An accident?" Saul shouted into the phone. "I'm on my way." James chuckled.

"I didn't even tell you what happened or what I needed." James replied as he rubbed his arm.

"You don't have to tell me, sir. You call, you need me, and I'm on my way." Saul hung up the phone abruptly. James knew Saul was a good friend. A loyal friend. He put the phone back down next to the sink and let his towel fall to the floor. He walked into the closet to find something easy to put on. He struggled to pull the sweat suit off of a high hanger, but he managed to get what he needed. Just as he pulled his underwear on, James could hear Saul coming through the front door. Saul must have hopped right in his car as he was hanging up. The steps got louder, and James began to move quicker to put on his clothes. But it was too late. Saul had already made his way into the bathroom and to the closet door. "Pastor?" Saul peeked his head into the closet door. "Hey Pastor. What's going on?" James walked towards Saul with only his boxer briefs and a white t-shirt on.

"I slipped when I was getting out of the shower, and I fell on my elbow. I didn't hear anything pop, but the pain is shooting all the way though my body, and I can't straighten my arm at all. I know something is wrong. I need you to help me get dressed and run me up there to the urgent care." Saul immediately picked up the pile of clothes laying on the floor next to James and sorted through them. He located the socks, got down on one knee, and motioned for James to pick up his foot to receive the sock. "I really do appreciate this man. I would have called Alice, but I didn't want to worry her. She's been having really great days. She's really starting to embrace this first lady thing." Saul then tapped the other foot for James to lift it for the other sock. James continued to talk while Saul laid his pants open for James to step in. "She's been lunching and shopping with the deacons' wives. I thought this move would be hard for her and the kids, but they're all adjusting so well." Saul pulled James' pants up around his waist.

"Do you want to put on your jacket now or do you want me to just drape it around you before we go outside?" James thought about it for a moment.

"Let's drape it. The docs will want to see the arm when we get there. It'll hurt too much to keep fiddling with it." Saul threw the jacket over his shoulder and motioned for James to walk towards the door. "Thanks again for this, man. I appreciate you getting over here so quickly."

"Stop thanking me, Pastor. I'm always here for you, sir." James looked at him strangely.

"Why are you being so formal with me?" James used his left hand to fake salute. "Yes sir. Sure Pastor." Both men laughed as they left the closet and headed through the bedroom and down the stairs.

"Do you have your wallet, pas-, um, James?" James scratched his head while he was thinking.

"I want to say it's in the car, but I'm not sure." James grabbed his keys from the table by the garage door and tossed them at Saul who caught them with ease. "Now that I think about it, I know it's in the center console. They both walked out of the door and Saul locked it behind them. James mashed the garage door opener on the wall and then made his way towards the passenger door of his car. That was an unusual feeling for him. Knowing his body was vulnerable was one thing, but his heart was hurting just as badly. "Hey man, can I share something with you?" James asked as he opened his door and got into the car. Saul got into the driver's seat and began adjusting the seat and mirrors.

"Of course. What's up?" Saul never looked at James. He just started the car and began to back out of the garage.

"I've been seeing Dr. Lily at the church." Saul stopped the car abruptly and looked James square in the eyes. It was so sudden that James hit his elbow on the seat. He screamed out in pain. "Hey!" He yelled at Saul. "Come on, man. I know it was a lot of information but, damn!

"I'm sorry. I wasn't expecting that at all. Based on some of your calendar meetings and late nights, I figured something was going on with someone, but I didn't suspect it was Lily." Saul pulled the car out of the driveway and headed down the road. "I wanted to date her, but she said I was doing too much at once. I guess she needed a little 'danger' in her life." Saul lifted his hands to do air quotes for the word *danger*.

"I swear I didn't mean for it to happen. I don't know what came over me. One day I was bringing in a program for our youth and the next I was falling in love."

"Love!" Saul half shouted. "It's been almost a year, but you're in love with her?" Saul covered his mouth in disbelief. "I mean, I guess she's a lovable person, but I'm really surprised. I thought you and Alice were couple's goals. Does she know?"

"Who Alice? Heck no! I've been trying to be the same husband to her. With all her ladies' lunches and social gatherings, she's hardly noticed." Saul continued to drive in silence for a while. James knew the news bothered him on several levels. He knew that Saul wanted to court Lily, but he also adored Alice. He'd always regarded Alice as royalty. The way she carried herself was likened to a British aristocrat in Saul's eyes. She was regal and to be put on a pedestal. "I'm not proud of myself, ya know." James looked in Saul's face for a reaction, but he didn't get one. "I've bungled this whole thing, but I'm not past the point of no return. I can fix this." Saul finally made a face.

"What do you need to fix? You said Alice doesn't know, right? And didn't Lily start seeing that dentist guy?"

"Yeah, but-" James tried to get his whole thought out, but Saul cut him off.

"No buts. Everybody's good." With Saul's declaration, his whole demeanor changed back to his normal, chill personality. He pulled into the parking lot of the urgent care building and drove directly to the roundabout in front of the door. "Go ahead and check in. I'll go grab us something to eat and meet you back inside. Judging by all the cars in this lot, it looks like we're going to be here for a while." James got out of the car and headed into the building. He was confused by Saul's reaction, but he didn't want to push his luck. It seemed like all was well, so James left it alone.

The Hard Choice

James had spent months watching Lily and Eric's love story unfold. She was glowing flawlessly as she and Eric only volunteered on the same days. James knew Lily avoided being alone with him since she met Eric. All communications and program developments came from a fellow doctor, never Lily. It was obvious Lily was protecting her heart and her relationship, but it never provided James with the closure he needed. He wanted to talk to her so badly. It burned his soul to know that he had hurt Lily, but his current agenda only held one action item. Apologize to Lily and clear the air.

As James sat in his office pushing his pen around making circles on notebook paper, his secretary provided a much needed distraction by knocking. "Pastor? Dr. Eric is here. He's requesting a moment of your time. I told him I'd see if you were free, and if not, then he could make an appointment for a later time. What would you like me to tell him?" James put his pen down as he thought. He'd never had a real conversation with Eric. They had exchanged pleasantries here and there the last few months, but they had never sat down for a real conversation. It would've been easy for James to just send him away, but he knew, at some point, he'd have to face this man.

"Let him in, please. Thanks so much." His secretary disappeared through the doorway. James sat up in his chair, adjusted himself to look more collected, and waited for Eric to enter. He realized he was posturing, so he sat back in the chair to look more relaxed. Eric entered the office with a smile.

"Good afternoon, Pastor. I apologize for popping in on you like this. I'm not scheduled to volunteer today, but I was in town, and I wanted to speak with you." He walked towards the desk and extended his hand for James to shake. James shook his hand and motioned for Eric to sit down across the desk.

"What brings you here to see me today?" James asked with a half-smile.

"Well, as you know, Lily and I have been seeing each other for a while. She's such an amazing woman, and I don't know how I was living life without her before. It's crazy how a good woman can do that for you. Am I right?" Eric chuckled to himself as he continued. "We've talked a lot, but in the midst of our conversations, I always felt like she was holding something back. Like she was never fully opening up to me. I felt like she wanted to, but I didn't want to make her feel uncomfortable by prying. Well, last night, she finally opened up. She told me everything." James took a hard swallow.

"Really? Everything?" Eric slid forward in his seat to close the gap between himself and the desk.

"Everything! I was quite surprised. A distinguished, accomplished doctor holding a secret like that? I understand why she'd want to keep a secret like this." James opened his mouth to interrupt, but Eric didn't let him. "I wasn't shocked though. Most women have an experimental phase in college, but I would have never suspected that Lily would be one of them." James' face went white and then flushed with embarrassment.

"Excuse me? Are you telling me that Lily's secret is a lesbian experience in college?"

"Yes!" Eric replied. "Kinda hot, huh?" Thoughts of beautiful Lily intertwined with another hot girl began to swirl around in James' mind. He could feel himself getting excited, so he had to change the subject. This couldn't have been what Eric came to tell him. He was confused and annoyed at the same time. Here he was trying to forget Lily and get back to his normal life and here comes this guy with nothing more than a bed of more distractions. Did he know what was really going on or was he still blissfully ignorant. At that point, James didn't care if it were the former or the latter. He wanted this guy out of his office.

"You couldn't have come all the way here to gossip about your partner. Am I missing something?" James stood up to allow Eric to excuse himself, but Eric remained seated. He motioned for James to sit down.

"No, I apologize. Sit down, sit down. I figured as a former professional athlete, you'd appreciate that bit of information. I'm sure you've seen and heard so much more. You may be a married pastor now, but I'm positive you have some war stories from the old days." James remained standing feeling himself getting angry. "I'll leave it alone. Let me get to the point of my visit." James sat down at the edge of his seat in case he had to get up again. Probably wanting to punch this rude asshole, but likely to show him the door. Eric continued. "I came here to ask if Lily and I could start a food pantry and soup kitchen out of the church's kitchen. We noticed you're only using it for the afterschool program and catering for weddings and repasts, but we feel like we could do some good in the community to improve healthy eating habits for better dental and overall family health. What do you say?"

James couldn't be more furious at this point. Here this guy is telling Lily's secrets, speaking for her as "we" knowing it was all her idea, and smirking in his face like the arrogant prick he was. James knew he could only respond in one way. He needed to calm down and make a rational decision, but he couldn't do it with this jerk in his office. "Let me speak it over with first lady and we'll get back with you. She's in charge of the kitchen and all its events. I'm not sure if she'll be thrilled about losing paid business for a permanent expense. She'll likely say no, so don't get your hopes up." James stood up for the final time to end the meeting. "I'll have my secretary call you to schedule a meeting when we have a decision." Eric stood up and extended his hand, but James didn't shake it.

"Thank you for your time, sir. Have a great day." Confused, Eric turned to walk out of the office. He paused at the door. "Did I offend you, Pastor? That wasn't my intention. Lily always talks about how down to earth of a guy you are, but I feel like I've given you the wrong impression. James could feel his sincerity, but he wasn't in the mood to make another guy feel better about his offensive actions.

"Listen, I'm really busy. I've heard your proposal and will get back to you as soon as I speak to my wife. Now if you'll excuse me, I need to get back to my sermon. I'm at a pivotal part that requires my undivided attention. God bless." Eric nodded in resignation and turned to leave. He took one last look at James, shook his head, and closed the door behind him.

Eric returned to the car with a defeated look on his face. Lily could tell his meeting with James didn't go well. He climbed into the driver's seat and immediately rested his head on the steering wheel. "He hates me." Eric declared.

"He can't hate you. He doesn't know you." Lily replied as she rubbed his back to comfort his bruised ego. "What happened? What did he say?" Eric lifted his head from the wheel to reply.

"I went in there, made some small talk like you suggested, and then asked him for the kitchen. He immediately got an attitude with me and said first lady is going to say 'no,' so don't get my hopes up." Lily sat back in her seat.

"First lady doesn't make decisions about the kitchen. He does. That's why you went to talk to him and not her. That's strange. Why do you think he had an attitude with you?" Eric laid his head back down on the steering wheel.

"He wouldn't even shake my hand on the way out. Told me he was busy and basically put his boot print on my ass on the way out the door. Babe, I don't know what I did, but that man hates me now. I don't know if he'll let me keep my program with the way he treated me today." Lily began to fume. She knew exactly why James was acting that way. He was jealous and was baiting her to come speak to him herself. She knew that would be a mistake. She knew that he was a twisted human being, but the rage that built up in her at that moment made her forget that she hadn't spoken to him in months. How dare he treat Eric in that way? She wasn't sure if she was in love with Eric, but she knew that she cared about his feelings.

"Give me a sec, babe. I'm going to have a word with the pastor. Would you mind running across the street and grabbing me a Reuben sandwich and some peach cobbler from the diner? Let's skip the fancy dinner, lay the diner food on the floor, and watch the game." Eric seemed to perk up.

"Yeah, that sounds like a plan. That's exactly what I need right now." He leaned over and gave Lily a gentle kiss and a one-armed hug. Lily smiled and opened her car door to get out. She closed the door and watched Eric put the car in drive and accelerate out of the parking lot. She then turned towards the church building. She knew this was a bad idea, probably the worst idea she's had in a while, but she needed to let James know that she was happy, and she needed him to put aside his childish ways for the good of the community. Lily had been asking Eric to spend more time in town with her, maybe even get his own place so she could see him more often. Yes, Eric had a successful dental practice in Gaffney, but she wanted him to be her full-time love interest in Charlotte. Having this program would at least put him in town every week. James was standing in her way and she wasn't letting that happen. It was the least he could do after Jackson. She gathered herself and walked up the church office stairs and into the building.

"Oh hey Dr. Lily." The secretary announced loudly. "That handsome boyfriend of yours was just in here. What brings you here?" Lily smiled as politely as she could to avoid the secretary knowing the kind of venom that she was about to spew at the pastor.

"Eric said he left something in Pastor's office. I told him I'd grab it for him while he goes to grab me some peach cobbler from across the street." The secretary smiled with all her teeth.

"Isn't that peach cobbler the best? I think I might get me some on the way home. Heck, I'm going to head that way now. Since you're going in to see Pastor, I doubt he'll see me tiptoe out of here a little early." The secretary started to gather her things.

"That sounds like a plan. Have a great night. Is it ok if I go in?" Without even looking twice, the secretary waved Lily on, pulled her keys out of her large, designer purse, and headed to the door. James must have heard the conversation because he opened his own door as Lily approached. Lily didn't miss a beat. "We need to talk. Now!" She declared as she pushed past him, bumping his chest with her shoulder. James stumbled back a few steps. Lily didn't care what kind of reaction he was going to have, but she needed to tell him everything that had been on her mind for the last few months and set him straight about how he treated Eric. At no point was she going to allow him to take control of the conversation or let him wiggle out of the accountability he needed to take for everything that transpired in Jackson.

"Lily? I wasn't expecting you. I'm glad to see you. I can see you're mad, but it's good to hear your voice say something other than 'hi' or 'bye' like you've been doing for months." Lily walked over to the far corner of the office and put her back against the wall. She needed James to see and hear her clearly, but she was also positioning herself defensively. Her back and shoulders were surrounded by walls, meaning he couldn't sneak attack her. She could see his every move in case he tried to approach her. She wanted total control in this room.

"Listen, this isn't a social visit. This is business. First of all, you need to know how much you hurt me in Jackson. You handed me out like a prostitute. That wasn't something I ever thought you were capable of, but I should have known better. Second, Eric and I are official and happy. We're a great team, he's not married, and I think I may be falling in love with him."

"Love!" James interrupted. "Come on Lily! You hardly know the guy. You can't be falling for that chauvinistic pig. You should have heard the way he was talking about you in here. It took me back to the locker room the way he was talking." Lily put her hand up to stop him.

"Not only was I not finished, but you're not about to insult my man. I think I would know if he were a 'chauvinistic pig' by now. Look! What we had was great. I really enjoyed the time we spent, up until the minute you turned into a pimp, but that's over now. Let's just agree to move on and let that be the end of it." James, still standing near it, slammed the door to his office shut. It startled Lily but she quickly composed herself. "Are we throwing tantrums now?" Lily asked sarcastically.

"This is some bullshit! I know I made a mistake in Jackson. Hell, I'm willing to admit that. But you can't be serious about this dude. He's not right for you." Lily felt herself begin to ignite. Who was this married pastor supposed to be, telling her who she should and shouldn't be with? Lily's voice came out swinging.

"You fucking hypocrite! Where do you get off telling me what to do? You want me to sit around and be your mistress forever. I've snatched a little bit of happiness for myself and here you come trying to ruin it. You're not concerned for me. You just want me to keep your secret. Don't you worry, Pastor, I would never expose you like that. But you need to let me live my life and run the programs that keep making you look good in the community."

"Calm down, Lily!" James warned.

"Don't fucking tell me to calm down."

"I said calm your ass down, Lily." James shouted. "Let me apologize and you can be on your way." James inhaled deeply through his nose and let it out through his mouth. "I'm sorry." James said softly. "It looks like you're happy now and our situationship is in the rearview mirror. Let's just shake hands and part ways as friends. Of course you and Eric can have the kitchen, and I'll even let Alice oversee all the volunteer activities so you won't have to see or speak to me if you don't want to." James opened his arms to offer a hug to Lily. "I promise. I sincerely wish you and Eric all the happiness in the world." Lily's eyes filled with tears. He seems so broken as he resigned. She couldn't tell if it was him realizing that they were officially over or if it was that he knew this would be their last conversation.

"Thank you. I accept your apology, but I don't think we can be friends. After everything we've been through, I think it's best if we keep things professional from now on." James continued to walk towards her with his arms out. Lily thought quickly. She thought about how this hug would be the last time she let him touch her. This hug would be the end of a months-long affair. This hug needed to be quick and dirty. No feelings, just a simple church hug. James wrapped his arms around her whole body and locked them behind her. He breathed in the scent of her hair one last time, and Lily could tell he was taking a sentimental moment for himself. She didn't want to rush his closure, but Eric would be back any minute. She needed him to let her go in more ways than one, so Lily folded her arms under and placed her hands on James' chest to push him back. She could feel his grip loosen and he let his arms fall by his side. She lifted her head to look into James' eyes. The tears began to flow between the both of them. James grabbed Lily's face and planted the most beautiful kiss on her lips.

"Good-bye James." Lily whispered as she stepped around him and walked out the door. She left James standing in the same spot. That was, in fact, the closure that they both needed. At least that's what Lily needed at that moment. She grabbed a tissue from the secretary's desk and wiped her eyes completely dry. She didn't need Eric to see she'd been crying. She was excited about their possibilities in life with this clean slate. James would be a thing of her past and Eric would be the man in her future. It felt like her past was a blur, but her future seemed clear. There wasn't a need to look back. Even though she could hear James' soft sobs coming from his office, she knew that nothing good could come from turning around. So, she walked out the door to the church office and never looked back.

James grabbed a tissue from his desk and wiped his face. He knew his work was done for the day. There was no way he'd be able to finish his sermon. He grabbed his keys and headed towards the door. As he grabbed the handle to the office door, he changed his mind. He needed some perspective before he went home. Alice and the kids were going to be waiting for him, so James needed a minute to clear his head. He walked back to the sanctuary door and walked through that one instead. He wanted to experience the quiet of the church from the pulpit. He walked over to the podium and looked out onto the empty seats. There, he could see all he had accomplished in such a short amount of time. He was now a megachurch pastor. People came from all over The Queen City to see him and hear him preach. There wasn't an empty seat in the house in any of his services on Sunday and even his Bible study was almost full. He had done what most people who started out in ministry couldn't accomplish in their entire lifetime. Sure, his previous celebrity had a lot to do with it, but it was his focus and tenacity that kept the people coming around week after week.

James turned around to the choir stand behind him. He leaned his head back, closed his eyes, extended his arms, and began to spin with glee. That's exactly the feeling of euphoria he needed to bring his life back into perspective. He had a loving wife and beautiful sons at home waiting for him. He knew what he needed to do. He needed to rededicate himself to his family. James stopped spinning and walked over to his seat. He sat down and laid his hands in his lap in the prayer position. He looked to the ceiling and began his declaration. "Lord, I thank you for everything you've done for me. It's been such a wild ride, and I pray that you guide my steps from here on out. Help me to be a better husband, a better father, and a better pastor to my flock. I pray that my life can be an example for others, and that the sins of my past will never come back to distract me again. I pray this in Jesus' name. Amen." James stood up, blew a kiss to the sky and headed towards his car. He felt relief in his prayer. He felt relief from his final kiss with Lily. And he felt optimistic about his future.

It didn't take James long to get home. He could hear laughter coming from inside the house when he pulled into the garage. He opened the door to a lively game of UNO coming from the kitchen table. Alice and the boys seemed to be having a spirited debate over the rules of the game. "Ok, we'll let dad settle this." Alice declared, as she motioned for James to come over. "Dad, can you put a Draw 4 on top of a Draw 4 to make the next person draw 8 or do you have to draw the original 4 and lose a turn?" James laughed because he and Alice had been playing the card game for years and could never agree on the rules. They didn't even bother figuring out the answer because the flirtatious banter always led to sex, so they never resolved the matter. But James knew the way he'd always played the game with his family and friends, so he could only weigh in on what he knew.

"I'm not sure if I should answer this question. You guys seem hyped up already. I don't want to start a riot. If you burn this house down, I'm sure the church is going to make us pay for it." Alice slapped James' arm.

"Answer the question!"

"Fine. I say, you can stack them. The next person has to draw 8 unless they have a Draw 4 card and so on." Alice screamed in agony as the boys cheered. She threw her cards at the table not caring where they landed.

"I QUIT! All y'all are cheaters." Alice pointed her finger at each person in the room. "You treat me badly because I'm the only female in the house. Y'all just wait until you get girlfriends, or better yet, wives. That'll even the stakes, and I promise the women will rule once again. Mark my words." Alice tucked in her finger and began shaking her fist at the boys. Her face was twisted in a wicked half smile and half vengeance smirk. She was joking, but everyone in the room knew she was seriously collecting the memories she would bring up in mixed company in the future.

James motioned for her to come here. Alice continued to make faces at the boys as she made her way to James. She looked at him inquisitively as James scooped her up in his arms. Her long legs dangled in the air. She turned her face into James' to take a kiss. The boys began to sing a chorus of disgust. James and Alice put their hands up to shield their faces from the boys as they continued to kiss. James walked them both past sets of twins to a hail of UNO cards and boos. Alice broke the kiss because she couldn't contain her laughter anymore. James put Alice down in front of the stairs. "Say good night to mommy." James declared as he patted her on the butt and motioned for her to go upstairs. He could tell that Alice was pleasantly surprised. They had made routine love for the last few months while he was seeing Lily, but he hadn't been this dangerous and exciting in a long time. The last time they made love while the kids were awake, it was a quick affair in the shower. This time they were being obvious and intentional with their actions. This didn't feel like a quickie situation and Alice knew it.

She trotted up the stairs with excitement and bounced through the bedroom door. She turned to face James, as he entered the room and closed the door behind him. "Where do you want it?" Alice asked as she began walking backwards, pulling her shirt over her head. James looked at her body from afar. He had forgotten how beautiful his wife actually was. He admired her for a moment as he pulled off his shirt in return. "Bed?" Alice asked. James shook his head to reject her proposal. "Shower?" Alice offered as an alternative as she took off her pants. James shook his head *no* again as he matched her actions. "Closet swing?" James knew that was her final offer, but that was the offer he wanted and accepted. He shook his head sexily as he bit his lip with pleasure at her. Alice turned and sprinted through the bathroom door and disappeared into their closet. As James rounded the corner, he saw Alice jump up and hit the trap door in their ceiling. Most women were too short or didn't have the free jump ability to do that, but James married an athlete who still had the hops to do that. That turned him on. Not only was he about to make love to his wife in a moment of rededication, but she was just as smitten by him after all these years.

"Damn babe. You can still get up." Alice laughed. She jumped up one more time to tap the door to the side and allow the sex swing to come tumbling down into position. It was obvious the swing hadn't been used in a while. The cloud of dust that came down with it was a clear indication that the swing had been collecting it for a while. James went into the bathroom to get a hand towel. He wet it and brought it back into the closet to wipe the dust from the swing. He found Alice tugging on it to make sure it was still secured to the load bearing beam. She stepped her foot into one of the straps and used her weight to hoist herself up.

"All secure." She smiled at James. She stepped aside to allow him to wipe off the swing with the towel. While James was distracted with his task, Alice took that time to remove her undergarments. She stood there eagerly naked and ready to mount one of her favorite sex contraptions. Alice purchased the swing and James mounted it years ago. They already had a vivacious sex life, so it was no surprise when Alice brought it home. They were about to christen it for the 100th or so time. James turned around to his delightful and naked Alice. "Ready?" She asked with glee.

"Ready." James declared. He helped Alice into the swing and took his boxer briefs off to match her nudity. It was like he was feeling her for the first time as James entered Alice's warm space. His knees felt weak as he moved with the motion of the swing. Alice moaned with pleasure as the aerodynamics of the swing provided all the motion to satisfy the burning desire within the husband and wife. It didn't take James long to realize he had lost control of his stroke. He was approaching climax and there may not be anything he could do about it. James closed his eyes tight to imagine something neutral that would help regain his masculine power. Alice looked into James' face with disappointment. She was so close to her elation, and she knew that look on his face.

"Don't stop, Marty. I'm gonna come." James immediately opened his eyes and backed his member out of his wife.

"Who the fuck is Marty?" The color drained from Alice's face. James turned and walked out of the closet as Alice quickly tried to escape the swing.

"Babe, wait." Alice called from behind him. "Babe, please. Let me explain." She continued to struggle, but James wasn't listening nor was he going to help her. He had to get out of there. He scooped up his pants and shirt from the bedroom floor and got dressed on his way down the stairs. He could hear Alice's voice in the distance, but he wasn't going to stop or respond. He could feel his throat closing and the oxygen leaving his body. He had to get some fresh air. He sprinted past the kids still playing cards and out the front door. He slammed the door shut and began to run down the street. James hadn't processed what happened just yet, but he knew he had to get out of there. All he could do was run. James ran down the street in his bare feet with no regard for his neighbors, oncoming traffic, or his own personal safety. Sure, he lived on a quiet street, but James wasn't in a state of mind to have rational thoughts. All he could think of was his perfect Alice screaming out the wrong name.

"Marty?" He said aloud. "Who the fuck is Marty?"

The End. . .

www.ingramcontent.com/pod-product-compliance
Lightning Source LLC
Chambersburg PA
CBHW071350170626
46811CB00003B/1072